W9-BMQ-257

A COFFIN FOR THE CANARY

Inspector John Coffin had a yellow canary — not a bird, but a woman, as the police refer to women who sing with a touch of hysteria. The beautiful Olivia struggles through a nightmare where fact and fantasy merge together in her disoriented mind as she tries to find out who really murdered her lover.

A COFFIN FOR THE CANARY

Gwendoline Butler

First published 1974
by
Macmillan London Ltd

This edition 2001 by Chivers Press
published by arrangement with
the author

ISBN 0 7540 8580 5

Copyright © 1974 by Gwendoline Butler

British Library Cataloguing in Publication Data available

Printed and bound in Great Britain by
Redwood Books, Trowbridge, Wiltshire

Chapter One

Before I knew what they were about they had me off the 9.20 train from Harrow and on to the train named Corruption. I say 'they', but these people had my co-operation. I played a great character in the plot of my own destruction. We all do, granted, but not everyone assists, insists, even, you could say, the way I did. I mustn't be bitter because I had, after all, had quite a lot of pleasure along the way. Or it seemed like pleasure at the time, the sweet and sour inevitably get mixed. I am the centre of it all, I thought, without recognizing my egotism. I am at the centre and the police and their investigation are peripheral. But shift the position a little and you will see the police are the hub and I am on the periphery, just a tiny object spinning round and round at the edge of a greater wheel.

Suddenly I realized I had a beautiful philosophical concept: the indivisibility of the human situation. I didn't know then that time too was a philosophical concept, and that it did not actually exist.

The train was crowded, but I had a corner seat with my heavy case perched precariously above. It was loaded with papers and books, not clothes. Nothing weighs heavier than paper, especially if it has the words of your life written on it. These did have. I've always been a compulsive diary keeper. One day I will re-read what I have written. I write in code, of course, not *en clair*, only a fool or an exhibitionist who wants the world to read does that.

5

But I can read my own code. How strange it would be if I could not. Imagine writing down words for ever after lost to you, like the day you have recorded. I might try writing in invisible ink. That way lies oblivion. My mind dwells on that marvellous thin ink. John Keats had the idea first, of course. Here lies John Keats, whose name was writ in water ... You know the rest. Only my chosen liquid would be not water but oil of vitriol, which would burn away the paper it was written on. I should lose everything that way and have nothing but my present to stand up in, which for a woman is a provocative and sexually interesting position to be in.

I began this particular journey there, although in a way I had been preparing myself for a long time. If I re-read my diaries, I expect I should see the signs. We do signal which way we are going, whether we know it or not. But naturally everything gets confused as events blend in. For instance, was it our first meeting or our second that we found we both loved films of the thirties and early forties? Films like *It Happened One Night* or *Mr Deeds Goes to Town* or *The Philadelphia Story*, some of which we had never seen and perhaps never would now, others we had seen at least twice. 'I always go at least twice, if I can,' he said. 'The first time just to see it and the second time for the detail and the technique.'

'Yes, it's the detail that draws me,' I confessed. 'The zigzag pattern on the cigarette George Raft pulls from his packet, the way the frilly cuff falls slowly off Joan Crawford's wrist. It's always the detail that counts.'

'I saw Jean Harlow in *Riff Raff* just once,' he said. 'It was in a little cinema off the Edgware Road and I was thirteen. It had a fire the next week and burnt down.'

'I tracked down a showing of Bette Davis and Leslie Howard in *Of Human Bondage* in a cinema in Dublin once,' I said. 'But by the time I got there the sound track had almost gone.'

Was all that the first time we met? Or the second? Certainly not the third time. It so happens I remember the third.

At the third meeting the room was dark and we didn't talk so much. I touched his shoulder under the sheet and it was warm and smooth.

'Listen,' I said, 'I've got to go and dress. I'll be back soon to say good-bye.'

You touch a person's shoulder and they feel normal and young, and, above all, alive. When you come back, hypostasis is already setting in. From being an object of desire and love, he is already transmogrified (an ugly word for an ugly state) by the due processes of nature.

Between one detail and another a whole life spends itself.

I had my diaries with me in the 9.20 train from Harrow Weald to Euston. I was moving a few remaining things from one house which had not been my home to another house which I had had for a few weeks, but which would probably not last long as my home either. My sister says I am not looking for a home. Otherwise, she says, I would have stayed with my first husband. I had three rooms behind their own front door in a house near Victoria Station. I always live near railway stations if I can. I like the sound of the trains. And then it's so easy to get away. Also, there is something about the proximity of a really major railway station that seems to bring the rents down. This was the first time I had been near Victoria and perhaps I wouldn't stay for ever. It was a temporary resting-place for me and my clothes and my papers. I had a telephone, so I communicated with my husband, and once in a while we met and occasionally he stayed the night. I didn't encourage it, but sometimes it happened and perhaps we were both the better for it in the end.

My sister said to me as I left, 'You know how to worry me. Somehow you get your blinkers on and then you move into trouble. I think you are in a blind spot now and moving fast.'

'What trouble have I ever been in?'

She gave me a long, long look and said nothing.

I sat in my corner reading. Opposite me were four people and beside me, three. Although I pretended to be reading Kurt Vonnegut I was taking in the appearance and manners of my companions, in the way known to all travellers who are curious but don't wish to seem so. It's really quite easy to read and stare at the same time. I've been doing it for years. But like so many things on this planet (I can't speak for the universe, which is too big for me) it works both ways, and it's as well to remember that. You are the observed as well as the observer.

I knew I was under scrutiny by the young man in the corner. I have been given the basic feminine training, which enables me to detect such inspection without loss of concentration.

At the end of the journey he knew something about me and I knew something about him. He knew I was coming from Harrow, I saw him reading the label on my case, which was an old one. He didn't know where I was going. About him I knew that he was travelling with one small case, but that it was very heavy; it strained his arms and shoulders as he lifted it down. I knew he had an envelope of papers he studied and then replaced in his pocket. I knew he had a glossy brown leather wallet which he fingered lovingly, quite unconsciously I'm sure.

There were two pale-faced men in the carriage. By the time the journey came to an end they, and the young man in the corner, and a motherly woman reading a magazine, were the only other people left in the carriage. We swayed and creaked the last few miles into London.

I stood up to get my case down. Before I could lay hands on it the young man had leapt to his feet and lifted it down. I smiled but said nothing. Closer to, I could see he was a little older than I had thought, probably about twenty-four or twenty-five. I saw the woman with the magazine give us a sharp glance. She looked again and then directly at me, just to make sure that I knew she was looking.

Quietly I moved along the corridor. I didn't want to speak to anyone. I wanted to be quite anonymous, quite silent. My tongue felt heavy in my mouth as if it didn't want ever to speak again. My tongue had worked over-time at the week-end anyway, talking with my sister. We don't quarrel but a certain amount of self-defence is necessary to both of us. Without saying a word we consti-tute an attack on each other, simply by living such very different lives. It looks as though there cannot really be room in the same world for both of us. That's how my sister seems to feel, anyway, and so when we meet she spends a good deal of effort trying to turn me into her. Bridging the gap, she calls it. There's no gap, though, it's a volcano.

The platform appeared and I stood by a door, my case on the floor, ready to move when the train stopped. The two pale-faced men stepped out from a door to my left and slowly paced down the platform to the street. They walked with an identical roll: you might have thought they were policemen except that they didn't look reliable enough. Modern policemen, perhaps.

I stepped out, and turned to pick up my case, but it was already in the hands of the young man. Silently he carried it down and handed it to me with a slight bow. I received it, possibly giving a slight bow back. It's so difficult not to imitate that sort of thing, isn't it? Then, as if he'd forgotten something, he turned back and thrust something into my hand and walked smartly away.

Mrs Motherly-face, who was just getting out, saw everything.

I opened my hand. In it there was a little bit of cardboard. I held it until I had carried my case out of the darkness of the platform into the lighted corridors that rose above the level where the train ran in, then I studied it.

Timothy Dean
Archibald Press

And then under and to one side his address:

24 Davenport Road, N.W.6.

Marvellous, I thought, a card. Who'd have ever thought he had a calling-card on him? It was a business-card, really, I suppose, but even that was a surprise to me.

There was some writing on the back. I went to get some coffee and toast for breakfast and I sat in a brightly lit plastic booth and read what he had written.

'I admire you, I want you. Will you come?'

Underneath he had written his telephone number.

What an unwise young man, I thought, to give his address and his telephone number to a stranger like that. And with such a message, written in pencil. I could blackmail him or something.

I suppose I had sat there for some time. A strange look must have appeared on my face, perhaps a forerunner of my deterioration, because a man sitting opposite leaned over and said, 'Are you all right, miss?'

'What?' I looked at him, seeing even the lines round his eyes, a pale-skinned thin man.

'Are you all right?'

'Yes. I'm all right, quite quite all right. I am between trains.'

Satisfied, perhaps even a little embarrassed, the man drew away. It was at this point I changed trains and put myself decisively on the train bound for downfall.

I drank my coffee and ordered an omelette to go with it, for I was suddenly very hungry. One appetite feeds another, no doubt.

I finished the omelette, drank some more coffee and put the card carefully inside my purse. I suppose it was a compliment he had written there, but I think my eyes behind their dark spectacles must have had a surprised and wary look. All the same I was triumphant. Well, good, I thought, he wants me.

I took a taxi to where I was living. I have a motor-car, but I had lent it to a friend. As I took out my key and let myself in I reflected that I lived not so far away from him. At a guess no more than six underground stations and another change of trains at Euston separated us.

I went inside and straightway saw a note on the table from my husband. So he too was thinking of me.

'Just dropped in,' he had written. 'I'd like to see you some time and talk. Maybe I'll telephone. But do you ever answer your telephone?'

I looked up from the note. 'Sometimes,' I thought. 'Sometimes I answer my telephone.'

But he had more to say. 'Lal was looking for you. Why didn't you say you'd be away? Please ring her.'

Lally, Louisa Alice Liliath Ashley, my best friend. I certainly would ring Lal, but with Lal you had to choose your moment. To begin with, she was hardly ever at home, and secondly, when at home, she always gave the impression of being immensely busy, although I never was sure what she was busy about.

I wandered round the place, tidying up. I had left in a hurry on Friday and the rooms had had all Saturday and Sunday to settle down into squalor. An untidy room left to itself for a few days can acquire an indiscriminate patina of neglect. I looked at the clock: nearly midday.

The telephone rang, and for a little while I thought no, I won't answer it. It stopped, was silent for a minute, and then started again. I picked up the receiver.

'Ah, I thought I'd get you that way,' said Lally's voice triumphantly. 'I knew if I stopped ringing and then tried again you'd never be able to resist answering. It aroused your curiosity.'

'Yes, it's as good a way of getting me as any,' I agreed. 'If I'm there. How did you know I was back?'

'Your husband told me he thought you would be. You two together again?'

'He was just guessing,' I said. 'But really we've never been apart. It's just it's less boring for us not being together all the time.'

'It seems to me you find him pretty boring even when he is there. Think he knows it, too, poor fellow.'

I didn't answer. I used to think myself he did really, but Lally was making things too straightforward as usual; boredom is often a mutual experience and I had every reason to believe I bored him too. 'It suits him,' I said. 'He likes it the way we do it.'

'And what makes you think he's going to go on liking it for ever?' said Lally.

'Reasons,' I said. There were none, really.

'Why aren't you answering your phone these days?' said Lally.

'I'm in hiding,' I said.

'I could believe you,' said Lally, doubtfully.

'Why not?' I said. 'It's a kind of a trick with me. Look

for the dishonesty. First I'm here, then I'm not. Why are you telephoning, Lally, what is it you wanted?'

'You're going to hate me, but it honestly wasn't my fault.'

'Go on, Lally, don't keep me waiting.'

'I've had one of my little patches of bad luck. You *know*, I lost a contact lens, burnt the cuff of my fur coat – it all started when I broke the mirror when I was shaving.' Lally was very superstitious.

'Do you shave, Lally?' I was interested.

'Only my legs. It's your car, love. I had it beautifully parked round the corner. It's been pinched.'

'Oh.' That was bad news, although it didn't make me hate Lally. I just wished it hadn't happened now. 'Don't worry, Lally, it certainly wasn't your fault. It could have happened to me.'

'I expect you'll get it back,' said Lally hopefully, 'and they can't make it any worse than it is, can they?'

'No,' I said.

'I mean, I can't think why they'd want to steal it, a beaten up old Bentley. I should think almost any other car would be a better nick.'

'You would think so, wouldn't you?' I said.

'You don't sound *worried*.'

'Oh, I am,' I said. 'I am.'

'That's it, then,' said Lally.

'When did the car go, Lally?'

'This morning. It was outside on the square last night and gone this morning.'

'Have you told the police?'

'No, I thought you could do that.'

'Yes,' I said. 'I'll do that, Lally.'

Then I told her about the man on the train and his open invitation.

'You wouldn't go,' she said.

'I might.'

'That's asking for trouble. As though you don't always.'

'You exaggerate.'

Lally and my sister ought to get together; they both seemed to hold similar ideas about my character. Where they differed was about my chances of survival. My sister saw no hope for me, whereas Lally, rather grudgingly, thought I would always come through. I wasn't entirely of Lal's belief myself.

When we had finished talking, I unpacked and made some lunch and ate it. Then I slept a little. It seemed to me I was tired and might become more tired. After I was rested, I tidied my room and went shopping. I don't eat much, but it isn't a habit I've entirely given up, and I needed one or two things.

While I was out I went into the delicatessen in the village. We call it the village, and it was one once, but all that is left of the village now is a small row of shops and a folk memory. And perhaps a degree of snobbishness. It sets us off from the rest of the area that we should be the *old* village. The delicatessen had an Italian name but was owned, I happened to know, by a wholesale grocer with his head office in Glasgow. The manager was called Fred.

I went in to buy half a pound of Mocha coffee and four ounces of Normandy butter. I came out with coffee, butter, a Camembert cheese, a slice of Brie, some smoked salmon, a tin of pâté and a good wedge of cheesecake. As well, I had a twist of bread flown in from Paris, a dozen eggs, three tins of soup and a melon.

'You're stocking up,' said Fred. 'Expecting a visitor?'

'I'm not sure,' I said. 'Maybe.'

'Well, all that stuff is highly expendable. Won't keep, you know.'

'No.' I stood on the pavement, feeling rather foolish.

No car and an armful of highly expensive short-life eatables. I went home and put them in the refrigerator. I had just about finished when I heard a key in the lock.

'I can't get used to you popping in and out like this,' I said. 'I haven't seen you for weeks, now twice in as many days. But at least there's plenty of food.'

'I want to talk to you.'

'You could have telephoned.'

'Thanks for the welcome.' My husband came in and sat down. 'You know, I like the way you've got things here. Did I ever tell you?'

'There's nothing to it,' I said, looking round. 'It's as plain as it could be.'

'Yes, that's what I like. It's sort of empty . . . as if you could move out tomorrow and it wouldn't matter. It means you're free.'

'I'm not free,' I said, turning away. 'Nor are you.'

'No. Just pretending.' He got up and started to walk round the room, eventually ending up at the window where he stood looking out. 'No. I'm not so free. I'm not sure I want to be. Olivia?'

'Yes?'

'Oh, nothing.' He stood there with his hands in his pockets, looking out. 'Well, Olivia, could we start up again? Would you come back?'

'I never really liked that place we had in Flood Street,' I said.

'We could find somewhere else. Or I could come here.'

I laughed. I had three rooms and the minimum of furniture, as he had already pointed out.

'I have one of everything here,' I said. 'And most of it plastic.'

'You planned it that way. That's what I mean by you being free. You could walk away tomorrow and it wouldn't matter to you.'

'I couldn't even drive,' I said. 'My car's been stolen.'

'Really? You do lose a lot of your personal possessions. Wasn't your bag stolen the other day?'

'Only lost,' I said. 'And it turned up.'

'So I take it the answer's no,' he said, turning round from the window.

'No,' I nodded.

'I'll say good-bye then.' He took his coat from a chair and walked off. 'It would have meant quite a lot to me, but if you won't, you won't.' At the door he paused. 'I'll let myself out. By the way, when you get the time, you might have a look from the window.'

When he had gone I went to the window and looked out. I could see him striding down the road. I watched him walk round the corner and I thought to myself, in Lally's words, 'And what makes you think he's going to go on liking it for ever?' Then I looked down at the kerb. There parked in the leaves and scraps of paper in the gutter, was my own old car.

I went to the telephone and dialled the appropriate number. He answered straight away.

'Hello,' I said. 'Is that Mr Timothy Dean?'

'Yes.' He knew who I was.

'I was ringing to see if you are at home.'

'I'm at home.'

'I'm coming to see you. Can I come now?'

'Please. Straight away.' He sounded breathless.

This was to be our first private meeting, on Corruption Day One.

Chapter Two

I knew he was dead by violence as soon as I saw him. There could be no question about it. Death by heart failure or some other natural cause was quite ruled out. Perhaps I cherished a hope that he had killed himself, that he had taken suicide for an easy way out, which it can never be. Perhaps he had in a way, inasmuch as I believe he had provoked death, but nevertheless it had not been *felo de se*.

It was murder. I could not escape the word, much as I wished. He had died by a gunshot wound, and there was no gun.

I knew I had to go to the police. I feared this visit but I knew there was no escape. One of the stops on the journey I had committed myself to make was a call on the police. It was a call of obligation.

I even knew the faces of the policemen I should see, their names and their faces. One was called Detective Inspector Idden and the other was Detective Sergeant Hodd. There was, I suppose, no reason why I should call upon these two men, of all the Metropolitan Police, with my terrible news. No reason except the realest reason of all: I knew that with whomsoever I started to talk and wherever I began I would end up talking to these two men. At first separately, as if they had no connection, and then together and then separately again. I had this deep conviction that whichever face I started with I should end up looking at theirs.

They had first come to see me about my motor-car. The one that was stolen. The only one I had ever owned. The bell rang just as I was going out.

'Oh, I'm sorry.' Without them saying a word to me I was on the defensive. 'Have you been ringing long?'

'Just a few minutes.'

'I was on the telephone. I suppose I didn't hear the bell.' And, of course, I didn't. I was far away, listening to the voice asking me to come to him straight away. What a marvellous beginning for a love story, I had thought. If it was to be a love story.

'May we come in?'

'But I'm just going out. Are you selling something?'

I knew they were not selling anything. They didn't look at all like sellers, nor buyers either, more like men come to price the goods.

The elder one smiled politely and introduced himself. 'We're policemen. I am Detective Inspector Idden.'

I stared.

'We've come about your car.'

'Oh, but it's back.' I was flustered. 'I know it was stolen, but it's been returned . . .' My voice died away. 'How did you *know* it had been stolen?'

He didn't answer the question. 'May we come in?' he persisted.

I held the door open and he walked in and the other one filed in after him. They went straight into the sitting-room.

'Is that your car out there?' he asked, going over to the window and looking out. 'The old Bentley? Number TWK 147D?'

'Yes.'

'Did you say it was stolen?'

'Yes, but I've got it back now.'

'So I see.' He turned back and looked at me and not the street for the first time. 'What's the story?'

'My car, which I had lent to a friend, was missing from some time last night until I happened to notice it not long ago outside in the square.'

'Hmmm.' He rubbed his cheek. 'So you didn't use your car between 8 a.m. and 12 p.m. today?'

'No.' I shook my head.

'And who was the friend you lent it to?'

'Miss Ashley. Louisa Ashley.' Lally under this name sounded a grand imposing person, quite unlike the Lally I knew, who, although I loved her, was feckless and unreliable.

He nodded briefly.

'But what does it matter?' I said. 'The car's back. I'm quite happy.'

'I'm not,' he said. 'During the hours you claim the car was stolen, a car with its description and bearing its number plate was used in a robbery on a post office.'

'Claimed?' I said. 'What does that mean? The car *was* stolen. Out of my use.'

I hoped to God Lally had been telling me the truth. She hardly ever lied to me.

'And then returned,' he said, glancing towards the window. 'That's certainly an unusual ending to the story.'

'I think you've got the wrong car.'

'That could be. We shall have to examine it, if you don't mind.' I shook my head. 'May we have the car keys?'

Lally had the keys, of course, unless she'd left them in the car, although she'd sworn she hadn't. 'I've got a spare set,' I said, going over to my desk. Silently I handed them to him.

'We may have to take the car away,' he said.

'Oh, but I'd like to use it.'

The other man, the Sergeant, hadn't said anything, but he had been taking in everything in the room. I could see he'd even read the date by which I would have eaten the carton of yoghurt on the table. I hoped it was a comfort to him. Judging by the flick-knife coming to irritable life in his superior's eyes he must often need comfort.

'A man was shot and may die as a result of what happened in the post-office raid,' he said. I thought they were a dodgy couple, but then I hate the police. I remember once when they arrested me, not this pair, of course, but their twin brothers, after a sit-in in Trafalgar Square, and the magistrates offered me the choice of twelve days or fifteen pounds fine. I chose imprisonment, naturally, and it was the police who pointed out that I had five pounds in my purse. The magistrates knocked off five days and took my five pounds. So they had me both ways. I didn't have another five pounds in the world at the time.

'You'd better take the car,' I said. It would be necessary to talk to Lally and find out what, if anything, she knew.

'Thank you. Of course, as soon as we can we will return it. If it turns out not to have been the car involved,' he said.

'It'll be the car involved all right. You'll see that it is.'

'What's that?'

'Nothing,' I said.

'Well, I have your address, Miss Cooper. And you've been away for the week-end, you said?'

'I didn't say, but I have. To my sister, who lives near Harrow. You can have her address.'

'Thank you.' He looked at the Sergeant, who wrote down what I had told him.

'Don't bother her, though, she's pregnant and has a sick child. I don't want her upset.'

'I won't unless we have to,' he said. 'And where is it

20

you work, Miss Cooper?' He looked round the room. I suppose he thought I *must* work. I couldn't sit in that dump all the time and look at my unpainted fingernails.

I took a deep breath. 'I'm Secretary to the Society for the Housing of the Helpless and Homeless. We call it "Shout".'

His nasty little smile flipped on and off. He knew the name all right.

'Well, one way and another, I shall know where to find you, Miss Cooper. There's no need to keep you now.'

I let them get clear away, and then I walked very slowly down the stairs and out of the house.

Sometimes I say things that are not true. That is, they are not true *yet*. 'I'm so worried', I will say when I am not particularly, or 'I'm in pain' when I can't feel a thing. But shortly I do feel the appropriate sensation, of pain, or sorrow, or even joy. I have known joy.

Now, as I hurried along, I found myself saying, 'I am very happy and I am very frightened.'

I wanted to get to him straight away but, in the first place, it wouldn't do him any harm to wait, and in the second place, there was a call I really must make. So I took a taxi and went straight to the Shout office, where they were just packing up to go home.

'Hello,' said Sarah. She is my assistant and sometimes my secretary. In a poor organization like ours she has to be both. She tried to pretend she was pleased to see me, but she wasn't, she just wasn't. I have known for a long time now that Sarah hates me and I don't know why. It's strange, because I like her and I am not used to being repulsed by those I like. She seemed particularly off me today; I could feel waves of irritation and dislike sweeping coldly towards me. 'Didn't expect you. Thought you had the day off.'

'I just dropped in to see if there was any post or any telephone call I ought to hear about.'

She gazed at me bleakly. She hated me to have personal mail at the office, as I frequently did. I don't think it was just curiosity, that there were letters she couldn't open, but more a sort of fury that I had a private life she didn't know about. I felt all this without being able to explain it : I wasn't in the least interested in *her* secret life. I expect she had one.

'No phone calls. There was a letter.' She reached for it and silently handed it over. 'How's your sister?'

'She's all right. More or less, anyway. Better than I expected really. She always picks up about the third month, and then sags again round the seventh. She's as gay as a lark once the baby's born, though.' I pocketed the letter without even looking at the envelope. In a remote kind of way I knew this infuriated her. 'She knows who it's from,' I could almost hear her saying to herself. 'She bloody well knows who it's from.'

'I suppose it's always that way,' said Sarah.

'Not with everyone,' I said.

'Ah, well.' She shrugged. 'We aren't really experienced, are we? I haven't had a child and neither have you.'

Much you know about it, I thought.

'No telephone calls?' I said.

'Only routine things I could deal with,' said Sarah. She was really looking tired and pale. I knew it was no good saying anything. Sympathy from me she did not want. Possibly it was the deep violet of the dress she was wearing that made her look pinched and plain. It was almost like being in mourning. I glanced at myself in the wall mirror and saw her looking at me too.

'That red suits you,' she said abruptly. 'Gives you a sort of glow.'

'Yes,' I said. But the glow didn't come from the dress

and I knew it and she knew it. It was funny how a time of buoyancy and happiness for me often seemed to be a period of depression for her. 'I'll be off, then.'

'I'm coming too.' She was efficiently locking up. We were the last people there and the rooms smelt smoky and fusty, with the air all used up, as they always did at the end of the day. Sarah yawned. 'It's been a day.'

'You're tired,' I said. 'I'll be back tomorrow. Why not have the morning off?'

'No thanks,' she said at once. 'I'll be in as usual.'

'And how was usual?' I asked, as we stood on the street.

'Awful,' she said. 'We had two families camped in the front office all the morning and most of the afternoon, telling us they had nowhere else to go but us. I thought they were here to stay this time, anyway for the night. They have done before now, and it *always* makes more problems than it solves.'

'I suppose one night under a warm dry roof is one night under a warm dry roof.'

'You think I'm heartless.'

'No,' I said. 'Not heartless, certainly never heartless.'

'Good-bye, good-bye, good-bye,' she said.

I walked off, thinking that the three good-byes must mean something. An abnormally high hope for my speedy departure, perhaps.

I found Davenport Road, which was exactly where I remembered it and where it had stood since its rapid and easy erection by a speculator-builder in the late 1880s. As a matter of fact, for the money, he had done a good job. His houses had stood intact through two world wars and still remained comfortable and easy living places. It wasn't a fashionable address, but it offered good, solid comfort. The address told me something about Mr Timothy Dean, although not enough.

He occupied a ground-floor flat. He appeared when I rang, although he made me ring twice.

'Hello,' he said. 'Hello. I thought you weren't coming.'

'Can I come in?' I walked past him. 'You didn't think I'd really come.'

'I wasn't sure.' His voice was husky. Attractively so, he probably smoked too much.

'You thought my phone call was the female equivalent of heavy breathing down the telephone line?'

He didn't laugh, but shook his head slowly. 'I didn't think you'd telephone and say you'd come unless you meant to come, but you were a long time getting here.'

'I was held up.' I looked about me. There was an ashtray loaded with cigarette ends, so he *was* a heavy smoker. The room was decorated in white and beige, the chairs covered in a rough tweed. In one corner was a deep jade green velvet chair and on the wall an abstract in tones of amethyst and soot. The whole effect was sophisticated and fresh. It told me rather more about Timothy Dean than I knew already. 'Of course, I could have been asking myself why I should come to you instead of you to me. Or why I should come at all. You were taking a chance asking me round here. Why didn't you ask me to dinner?'

'I didn't dare do that,' he spoke seriously. 'You might not have come.'

'You still don't know where I live.'

'No. I don't want to.'

'I'll think about that,' I said, after a pause. 'And if I ever come up with what could be your reasons then we'll have a discussion on it.'

'It's just a feeling I have.'

'And your other feeling was that you wanted me?'

'Yes.'

'Now I know why I came round here,' I said, getting up. 'It was curiosity.'

I walked towards the door but I walked quite slowly and I don't think he thought for a second that I'd really go. Anyway, he didn't move but just watched me silently.

'Well, aren't you going to open the door for me?'

'No.' He shook his head. 'That was an awful train, wasn't it?'

'It seemed all right to me.'

'No, it smelt of fish and it was dirty.'

'I thought you were watching me?' I was a little piqued, ridiculous of me, but I was. If he was thinking of me he shouldn't have noticed that the train was so bad.

'That's why I started to look at you.' He smiled. 'You were the prettiest and freshest thing in it and I thought "I wish she was mine. If she was mine it would make up for a lot."'

I was touched and a little troubled. I didn't want him to really care about me, not in any way except the lightest, the most passing way.

'I wish you hadn't noticed me,' I said.

'But I thought you wanted me to. I thought you were looking at me, too.'

'I was looking at everyone in the carriage.'

'Yes, so you were. I saw that, too.' He laughed. 'Terrible, weren't they?'

'Yes.' I had no doubt about that simple fact. It was a good word – terrible.

'Let's have a drink.' He started to open a wall cupboard which was disguised as several rows of books. It was quite neat. I wondered if there were any more little hidey-holes in the room.

'No.' This time I took hold of the door-handle quite firmly. 'I think I'd better go.'

'Oh no, please. Why?'

'I came here to find Timothy Dean. I think I've found him,' I said.

'Well, have one of Timothy's drinks before you go.' He smiled as if he'd made a joke. 'It's all right, you know, I won't ask you to stay after you've finished it.' He was standing gazing at the sophisticated selection of drinks that the cupboard contained. He looked as if he didn't quite know his way around it. *Not* a drinker, I thought, in spite of the array of bottles. Someone had drunk from them, though, as all the bottles were opened. 'You know, I'd feel a bit insulted if you went without a drink. What would you like?'

I decided to stay. 'There's gin in that anonymous-looking bottle,' I said. 'I'll have some of that, with bitter lemon.'

'Yes, it is gin.' He was pouring it absently. 'Thanks for staying.'

'I don't know why you are thanking me.' I took the drink.

'Of course I'm thanking you for coming and I'm thanking you for staying.'

'I don't believe I'm what you think I am. I believe if I stayed for long enough you'd be disappointed in me.'

'Stay here and try,' he said. 'At least I'll have your company.'

Although he placed no special emphasis on these words, and even smiled as he said them, I sensed they meant something to him.

'Are you lonely, then?'

He nodded.

'But you have a job. You're successful, too.' My eyes wandered round the room. It was full of expensive objects. 'You can't be that lonely.'

'There's a special kind of loneliness.'

'What sort of a publisher are you?'

He stared at me.

'Publisher. Archibald Press. Your card,' I said.

'Oh.' He laughed. 'Oh, they publish text-books on scientific and medical subjects. Also legal subjects. And they are branching out into art history.'

'And what do you actually do?'

'I drum up custom for them.' He sounded offhand.

'Booksellers and readers?'

'Yes. And then on the other hand I persuade people to write the books. Got to actually have the product before you can sell it.'

'You must be a doctor or scientist then,' I said.

He looked at me alertly, as if I'd made a great discovery. 'Why?'

'Well, obviously you have to know about the product,' I said.

'I'm not a doctor,' he said.

'Do you know, I get the impression that you're not dead keen on your job.' I sipped my drink. 'No, you sound a little far away and detached about it.' I hesitated. 'Is that why you are lonely?'

'Yes, yes, I suppose it is. Lonely and afraid.'

The little word dropped into the world from space and could not be hauled back.

'Afraid?'

He got up. 'Forget I said it. It was a silly thing to say. It doesn't mean anything. After all, plenty of people have little private areas of fear they don't want to be too specific about.'

'Plenty,' I agreed. 'And most of them are receiving treatment for it.'

He laughed. 'I'm not mad.'

'I think you're very rash,' I said slowly. 'I think you do very imprudent things. Like scribbling that message on your card and pushing it in my hand.'

'You know what?' he said. 'I think *you're* very rash. I think you do imprudent things. Like coming in response to what I wrote on that card.'

'That makes two of us,' I said, taking a drink. 'An inflammable combination.'

We were travelling quite fast on our little journey towards dying, he and I. Perhaps he was going faster than I was. But there can never be any doubt that we shall meet up at the same point in the end.

> The grave's a fine and private place
> But none I think do there embrace.

But that's just my point, they do. We shall.

'I'm terribly glad you're staying,' he said. 'I feel much safer now you're here. Stay and stay, won't you?'

'I *could* stay for ever,' I said. 'I've just left one home. The new one I've got is nothing much. I could forget it.'

This would put some people off, perhaps I half intended it should, but he went on being delighted.

'Yes, stay for ever.'

'I might get hungry,' I said hastily.

'I've got food for ever.' He went to a door and revealed a kitchen, and I could see he had indeed got it stocked with tins and tins of food. 'There's more in the refrigerator,' he said.

I laughed. 'You could stand a siege in here.' I thought it was time to go.

'Yes, and with you for company.'

'But I am not about to be walled up with you.' I finished my drink and stood up. His hand detained me.

'You've only been here twelve minutes. I've watched the clock.'

'There isn't a clock in here,' I said, looking round. 'I've noticed.'

'It's the clock inside me.'

'An unreliable timepiece,' I said dryly. It wasn't one I wanted to live by in any case.

'Tick tock, tick tock. I'm a clock.'

'Bombs make that sort of noise,' I observed.

'Yes.' He stopped laughing at once. 'So they do. I suppose I could explode, too. But I won't do it without warning.'

'Thanks,' I said. 'I won't wait, though. And don't put anything off for me. If you want to explode you go ahead and do it.'

'It's better with company.'

'Yes,' I said. 'That's what's making me nervous.'

'You *are* nervous. I thought you were. You, for instance, you keep looking out of the window.'

I was looking out of the window to see if I'd been followed. I didn't think so, but I wasn't sure.

'Tell me the truth. Why did you really ask me to come round here?'

'I thought you wanted me to. I saw you looking at me. You *did* look?'

'Yes.' I nodded.

'You did want me to take notice of you. To make a move towards you.'

'In a way.'

'You were interested in me,' he persisted. 'I could tell.'

'Yes, I was,' I admitted. 'In a way.'

'I suppose that's how it happened, then. That's how it always starts. It doesn't have to end there, though.'

'Tell me more about your publishing,' I said abruptly. 'Tell me what you do and how you do it.'

'It's a job like any other.'

'It seems to produce a good spending power,' I said, looking round me.

'Oh.' He too had a look round. 'Yes, I suppose it does.'

'Don't you *know*?'

29

'I have a little money of my own.'

'Well, that's nice,' I said. 'You're not a secret million-aire, are you?'

'I can see you despise me for it.'

'Not at all. There's always a point in the film where someone, it's usually the female star but it can be the male star, confesses that they are not what they seem. Either they're richer or poorer, or they're blacker or they're whiter. It doesn't matter which.'

'They haven't been making that sort of film for years,' he said.

'Never mind. Our culture is founded on them. We're living out that myth, you and I, thinking that sooner or later we will find someone to surprise us.'

'People can do that all the time,' he said.

'That quite ordinary people have the capacity to change the course of the action, to provide a solution,' I went on, '*that* is what we believe in.'

Was it then we started to talk about Bette Davis, or was it the next time? One episode swims into the next. But I know it was soon that I said softly. 'Now tell me the truth about why you asked me to come. Underneath the obvious reason, why did you ask me to come?'

'You're still looking for that secret hero?' he said, drawing back a little. I hadn't realized till then how close we had drawn together.

'Yes,' I admitted.

He took a deep drink. 'Very well, I'll tell you. I didn't want to be alone tonight.'

'Why not?'

'It's my birthday. I was born about two o'clock, I be-lieve. Anyway, that's the legend. So my birthday starts a few hours from now.'

'I'm interested in your use of the word legend,' I said curiously.

'I shall be twenty-six. That's the age fatal to genius. Keats, Shelley, one or two others. They ended there. I once made a vow that if I *did* live to be twenty-six I'd kill myself then.' He looked quite serious.

I was silent for a moment. 'How old were you then?'

'Fifteen. But, of course, I don't still want to do it.'

'That's all right, then.'

'But I don't want to be alone, tonight,' he said urgently. 'I want you to stay with me to see I don't do it.'

'I issue a dispensation.' I stood up. 'I, Olivia Cooper, by virtue of the authority vested in me, declare you free of your vow.'

'But I want you to stay. I don't want you to go. I don't want to kill myself.'

'I know you don't. But I've explained: you're in the clear.' For extra reassurance I added: 'In any case the age reputed to be fatal to genius was thirty-seven, not twenty-six, so you've got another eleven years.' Eleven years before he joined those illustrious ghosts, Caravaggio, Mozart, Raphael, all dead at thirty-seven.

'I shall feel safer with you here.'

'You know,' I said, 'if this were an A film, what you'd really be wanting would be for me to do the job for you.'

'That's not vintage film stuff, is it?' he said regretfully. 'More like mid-fifties. Say French or Swedish.'

'There's another twist,' I said, watching his face. 'I just thought of it . . . You *think* you're the one who's looking for a hiding-place. It could be me. In this plot it is me.'

'Go on,' he said. 'I'm interested.'

I went to the window for another look. 'You *could* be hiding a fugitive from the law.'

'What law?' he said quickly.

'The usual sort, you know. The Queen's writ runs here.'

'Oh yes,' he smiled at me. 'Well, I don't mind giving you sanctuary.'

'It may not come to that.'

'What's the charge?'

'The police say my car could have been used in an armed robbery.'

'And was it?'

'I think it may have been,' I said carefully. 'The police think so, anyway. It was out of my possession at the time.'

'Then it's nothing to do with you.'

'No, I can't get out of it as easily as that. A man was shot, you see. It's my car. There is a connection.'

'Have you got the car still?'

'The police have it.'

'I expect they'll give it back.'

'Oh, in time, in time.' I got up. 'Well, good-bye, good-bye.'

'I think you've invented that story about the car and the robbery.'

'No, what I'm telling you is quite true. Two policemen called and asked me questions.'

'But were they really policemen? You have to be careful, you know.'

'Oh, they were real policemen. But what their real purpose was – I'm not sure.'

'You mean it wasn't true about the car?'

'Oh yes. I'm sure that part is true. I think they told me the truth. Of course, it wasn't the whole truth. It never is. Between one detail and another detail could be another whole story.'

'Yes.' He sounded worried. 'Might be nothing to do with you, though.'

'It *is* something to do with me. There's a story, and it's about me and I don't know how it reads.'

'You could try guessing. You must have somewhere to start.'

'Yes, I *do* have a starting-point. I lent the car to my best friend. I might try asking her. It was stolen when she had it.'

'You don't think *she* robbed the bank?'

'Oh no, no. But why did it get stolen when she had it and not me? And why did it come back to where I live?'

'Did it?'

'Yes. My husband looked out of the window and there it was.'

'Perhaps your husband brought it back.'

'The thought did cross my mind. But he never robbed a bank in his life. He's a most respectable man.'

'Does he know someone who would?'

'I don't think so.'

'Do you?'

'It looks as though I do,' I said sadly.

'I'm interested in your husband.'

'Oh, don't be. He's not very interesting. Boring, really.'

'Why did you marry him, then?'

'I suppose at the time I liked the idea of someone boring. It seemed what I needed.'

'But it wasn't enough?'

'It never is, is it?' I asked.

'Do you know, I believe you're as lonely and looking for company as I am. You wanted to come here if you could.'

'If I could,' I admitted.

'You wanted in . . .'

'Well . . .' I hesitated. He put one hand on my leg. It was long and sun-tanned with very very short blunt nails. His hand felt thick and warm on me. 'There's something wrong with your hand,' I said.

'No, not really.'

'But yes.' I turned it over. On the palm right across it from the base of the thumb to the little finger was a thick plaster.

'You could feel that through your stocking?'

'Yes. It burned me.'

'It can't possibly have done.'

'But it did.' I held out my hand. 'See, I feel it.'

'Yes. Now you're burning me back.'

'I know.' I could feel my heart banging.

'You won't go away? You won't leave me? Or at any rate, not now? I need you.'

'Oh yes?' I said. I have a piece of steel inside me that I keep specially sharp for occasions like this. 'I've heard that before. And I always wonder what it means.'

'With me it varies from place to place and person to person,' he said politely. 'I'm not an easy person to know.'

'I've already discovered that. I feel I need to know a lot more about you.'

And so I stayed that night. In the middle of it I awoke and gazed into the half-lit room with its expensive furniture muddled by our living in it. I felt it was a room meant to be empty. *He* was asleep, for the moment, relaxed and quiet.

I raised myself on one elbow and looked down at him for a moment. Although I thought he breathed, he looked white and dead, as if I had drained him of life. 'Yes, I'm the blood-sucking type all right,' I thought as I turned over on my side and closed my eyes.

That was the first time. I said good-bye to him while he still had his eyes closed.

'Good-bye,' I said, leaning over and touching that still warm shoulder. 'I saw you through the night, anyway.'

'Did you find out all you wanted to know?'

'Some. Good-bye. Don't go out. Stay home and keep warm and I'll be back by evening.'

'You look like Lana Turner this morning.'

'Not a hope,' I said. 'It's a different kind of film altogether and we really only meet face to face in the last reel.'

'How can that be?' he said sleepily.

'It's one of those trick camera techniques,' I said. 'Good-bye.'

Early in the day, before going to work just after leaving home, I had an idea and in pursuit of it I caught a bus and travelled a short trip across London Bridge, south of the river. Two friends of mine, David Short and Tony Tomlinson, ran a small local newspaper. They were lucky it hadn't been snapped up by a big chain of newspapers, and the reason it hadn't been snapped up was that there was so little to snap. But the proprietors had big ideas. They were hoping to turn it into a sort of weekly obligatory reading or a Do-it-yourself Ombudsman. All the polite little scandals and muddles of bureaucracy were to be aired each week. The groundwork for this made an excellent intelligence service necessary; I knew they were building up a network of informers.

'Oh, hello, love,' said David. 'Wanting us?'

'She always does, don't you, Olivia?' said Tony. Since I saw him last he had grown a long droopy moustache which made his gentle obstinate face look older and sadder. Some freak of nature had blessed his moustache with auburn hair which glistened in the sun; his own full flowing locks were quite black.

'The police think my car has been used for an armed robbery. I want to know what evidence they have. If any.'

'Do you suspect the police of faking it?'

'No. I think they must have something. My car must have been seen. May have been used, even. I want to know the truth of it.'

'You need a detective for that,' said Dave.

35

'No. I can't afford it. I won't have anything to do with a private detective.'

'I can find out what the police themselves think,' said Tony suddenly.

'*Can* you? How?'

He shrugged.

'Yes, I know,' I said. 'Ask a silly question!' So somewhere there was a policeman who was observing his colleagues and not feeling quite at home with them. The part of him that could not settle in the Force could reach out and talk to Tony. You couldn't assume that after such a talk he would be the less of a policeman; he might be more of one. Tony had no fixed attitudes himself, and had a way of strangely settling you in your own.

'Find out if you can,' I said. 'Don't press it. I don't want to be a trouble.'

'For us you're never that,' said David. However, I had been a trouble to them in the past and would be so again. I won't call it fate, but it was written into the script. They would regret that they knew me.

'Shall I ring you if I get anything?' asked Tony. 'Or will you call?'

'I'll call. I'm not sure where I shall be. I move around. How long shall I give you?'

He thought. 'Try me tonight. I might be able to help then. Information will either come quickly or not at all in this case, I think.'

I thanked him and left. I went into my office and worked with Sarah, whose mood seemed bad. In the middle of the morning my husband telephoned and asked me to meet him.

'I won't suggest anything as civilized as lunch,' he said. 'I suppose you're on one of your not-eating kicks. You looked as though you were.'

'I'm not hungry much these days,' I admitted. I was

eating all right, though. I strongly suspect I was eating bits of myself. Nothing very much, you know, a mouthful of backbone, a little bit of mind. Somehow, of course, a few bites of other people got mixed in. 'You can buy me a drink if you like.'

'You looked terrible yesterday.' He kept on and on. He always did.

'Don't growl,' I said. 'What's it to you?'

'You're still my wife.'

'Just. Barely.'

'We could make it more.'

I was silent. I could see Sarah looking serious across the room, so I smiled at her. She nodded slightly. Another bad day for her today. 'I'm happy the way things are,' I said, staring into Sarah's sombre face.

'I'll see you tonight, then,' he said abruptly. 'I'll call for you at your place.'

'You know there's a committee meeting,' said Sarah.

I made a face. I am obliged to attend such meetings, although I regard them as a waste of time.

'So there is, and I wanted to see Lally.'

'She's been ringing you,' said Sarah. 'Well, you *were* late in.'

'So I was.' I didn't like the sound of Lally in search of me, it sounded like more trouble about the car. 'Did she say anything?'

Sarah shook her head. But I got the feeling she wasn't being entirely truthful. She and Lally had an underhand way of talking about me when I wasn't there. It never failed to annoy me when I found out about it afterwards, as I nearly always did from Lally's habitual lack of caution. I found out just enough to make me wonder about what went on on all those other occasions when I never got to know what Lally and Sarah told each other about me.

'Well, I don't think I'll do anything about her,' I said thoughtfully. 'I'll just leave her to find me.'

'Do you want me to pretend to her that you are out?' asked Sarah.

'No,' I said, 'but I might ask you to telephone my husband later and say I've been called away and can't meet him tonight.'

'He'll be upset,' said Sarah.

'He might be more upset if he actually gets to see me,' I said. Sarah smiled. It seemed at last I had actually made a joke she could laugh at.

I worked for half an hour, then rushed off to the committee meeting, which was held in a decrepit room on the floor below. Except for us, the whole building was empty and due for demolition. We rather specialized in buildings of this sort. At first I'd hated it and was always washing my hands. I'd got used to it now and no longer minded being dirty. I still minded being damp and cold, though. We were always damp and cold.

I sat with the committee and took notes. Our chairman was a famous figure, a writer and a poet. It would be smart to say that I found him, behind the celebrated charm, a phoney. But it wouldn't be true. I thought him a nice man and absolutely genuine. He worked hard for this cause in which we all believed (me less than the others, maybe). I've believed in so many things in my time that it's become a habit which is wearing thin. I no longer believe in myself, you see. and in the end this is what matters. So we all believed in the cause, but we were so ineffectual. We made brave noises about being a pressure group and forcing the government to notice the problem and take action. And the government did notice and did take action. But what we really needed was the millennia to roll away and solve our problem for us. In short, we needed an act of God, and God wasn't available. So far as I could see, his line was permanently tied up. You could try it, but you always got the 'busy' signal.

In my small way I did sometimes go round taking God's function on myself and blowing up bits of the universe, and this was why the police didn't like me and our famous chairman, a real man of peace, didn't trust me. He was eyeing me warily now, for which I did not blame him.

We were a wordy lot. We broke off the meeting at midday for something to eat and then went back to it afterwards. We went on and on, so that I was behindhand for the rest of the day and never got in touch with either Lally or my husband.

There was a scribbled note from Sarah on my desk, which said Miss Ashley telephoned and said would you please ring her at the Parade office. Parade was the boutique where Lally, whose own clothes were a joke, did the accounts. These were probably a joke too, although possibly not a very good one for Parade. I looked at the clock and guessed that Parade would be closed. Lally might still be there, hanging about by the telephone and waiting for me, but not very likely.

I walked to the tube station and pushed through the rush hour crowds to my own train. I suppose I did look around when I emerged, in the way one does, to see if there was a face I knew, but I don't remember taking any other precautions. It was still early evening, plenty of people about, I didn't have a twinge of fear. Naturally I had noticed two men walking behind me, but I thought nothing of it at all: not until I was in the house and had closed the front door behind me to walk to my apartment and then heard it close again.

I turned round when I heard the footsteps and drew my breath sharply. *Now* I was afraid. There were two men and their faces were covered with nylon stockings. One of them jumped two steps like an animal, grabbed me by the waist and put his hand over my mouth. He had on thick leather gloves. I choked, and he lifted his hand just slightly from my lips.

'Don't try shouting,' he said. I glared at him over the glove. The other man came up behind and between the two of them they bundled me up the stairs to my own front door. It lay back in a small recess, and this was where they took me and stood me up against the wall. The gloved hand came away from my mouth.

'Still don't try shouting.'

I took deep shuddering breaths. 'If it's about my car,' I said. 'I didn't . . .'

I couldn't finish. One of them, he who had on the leather gloves, poked me in the diaphragm, silencing me and winding me. 'If we ask you to do anything, then do it,' he said. 'Remember that. If we come here and ask you to do anything, do it.'

'Say yes,' said the other man.

'Yes,' I said, as soon as I could speak.

'If the police ask you about your car, remember you *said* we could use it.'

'No,' I gasped.

'It's the truth. You gave us permission. That makes you an accessory. You're in, baby, in.' His sick, silly voice died away. I think there was something else. I heard his voice contriving to speak, but I could not seem to take it in.

The man with leather gloves removed his hands and I slid to the floor. I was furious with myself for being so weak. I remember rubbing my left arm.

I heard them run down the stairs and then the front door banged. I lay on the floor feeling terrible. There was a warm little trickle from my nose and when I raised a hand that still trembled to investigate I found my nose was bleeding. I suppose that at some point in the pro-

40

ceedings my face had got banged. Was there something I had forgotten?

My husband came up the stairs to find me still on the floor and fumbling for my handbag.

'What on earth's happened to you?' he said. He put his arm round me and led me in.

'Whatever it looks like, it's not rape,' I gasped.

'My God, if that was all, it would be easy.' He sat me down and went to get me a drink.

'That's what you think,' I said. 'A typical masculine reaction.' I sipped the drink and felt better.

I left him and went to the bedroom and cleaned the blood from my face and combed my hair. I put some lipstick on and then took it off again. There are times when the face looks distinctly worse with make-up than without, and this was one of them. It's as well to recognize these moments.

'You look better now,' said my husband, as I came back into the room. He gave me a quick glance and then turned away again. He was embarrassed by me today for some reason. He never liked to stare trouble in the face and I suppose I was just that for him.

I sat down in a chair and steadied my breathing. I was amazed how calm I felt. The two men could have killed me, but they hadn't. Perhaps they would next time.

'Now what did happen?' said my husband. 'And don't tell me nothing did.'

'Two men followed me into the house when I came in and attacked me.'

'What did they do that for?'

'I'm not sure but I think it may be connected with the theft of my car.'

'Seems funny.'

'It's the only thing I can think of. The car was stolen and seems to have been used in a robbery. The police think I know something about it. Perhaps these men think I do too, and want to keep me quiet.'

'Still sounds funny. How did they get in?'

'You know that door. It's not kept locked.'

'True enough. Well, I don't like it. Want me to telephone the police?' He was already half way to the telephone when I reached out a hand.

'Don't. I've had all I want of the police at the moment.'

'They *ought* to know.' He was shocked at me.

'What can they do? The men have gone, the police won't find them.'

'You could give the police a description.'

'What of? Two men with heavy hands and masks on their faces?'

'They were masked?' He gave me a strange look at this.

'Well, nylon stockings. Horrid things.'

'Nothing spontaneous about this attack, then. You didn't just blunder into their path this afternoon and get beaten up for your pains, they had it planned.'

'You know, they didn't really hurt me, they just frightened me.'

'Look.' He came and sat down beside me and took my hand. 'You're my wife. I feel responsible. I can't just stand by and let you be attacked and do nothing about it.'

I felt sad at this, he was such a good man, much too good for me.

'Let's write it off to experience,' I said, withdrawing my hand. 'They wanted to frighten me and they did frighten me. I admit to the experience. What I shall do about it? I don't know. Nothing, probably.'

'I still think we should tell the police.'

'Perhaps they were policemen,' I said.

'Surely you don't mean that?' He was horrified.

'The police don't like me very much,' I said thoughtfully, 'and I *do* mean that. And not all policemen are kind men with white gloves, far from it.'

'It's the masks,' he said. He sounded hopelessly confused. 'I can't believe the police would wear nylon stockings.'

'Why not? Do you think they'd want me to get a good look at their faces?'

'You horrify me.' He threw himself into a chair, and stared at me. 'Can you really believe it was the police?'

'I said two policemen, not the police. I'm not suggesting it was an official section. No doubt they were acting on their own.'

'You're mad.'

'I'm just throwing around ideas. I'm open to other suggestions.'

'You've got your colour back.'

'Yes, I feel better now. What did you want to talk to me about?'

He stood up. 'I'll take you out for a meal.'

'You always save up bad news for food.'

'That's not true. You look as though you could do with a good meal.'

'I *am* hungry.' I was surprised at myself, but it was true. For the first time in weeks I wanted to eat. 'Nowhere expensive, though.' I was feeling better, ready to relax. Why then at the back of my mind did I seem to hear a voice shouting, 'Liar, liar'? I looked down at my arm, on which had appeared two tiny pricks like a viper's kiss.

'Of course not.' For the first time that evening he relaxed and let himself smile. 'I know better than to try to raise you above subsistence level.'

At dinner, when my hunger had been satisfied and I was drinking coffee, he said: 'That joke you made, about it not being rape. It *was* just a joke, wasn't it?'

'I don't think sex entered into it.'

'With you it usually comes in somewhere,' he said, half under his breath.

'Here and there, it does,' I said, 'but you've got to remember it's never the important thing.'

He flushed; he didn't like me saying it, and was angry, which was what I intended.

'You had something to say to me, I think?' I said.

'I have a formal proposal to make.'

Something about the way he said it alerted me. I could predict what was coming. Some lawyer had put those words into his mouth.

'If I take the lease of a new house, a new place to live, somewhere we can make a home, will you join me there?'

I always had to remind myself that he was relatively rich, and that he could buy new leases and invest capital in expensive freeholds as he wished. I had enjoyed my short life as a full-time wife with a freedom to spend at Harrod's and Fortnum & Mason and to buy my clothes from Yves St Laurent. But I am not naturally a dweller in such rich territory, and I had not minded leaving it behind.

'No, thank you,' I said. 'In many ways it's a nice idea, but we tried it once and it didn't work. I didn't feel myself, somehow. Can't we leave things as they are?'

'I don't think so. I should like a divorce.'

'Of course. Arrange it as you like. I will co-operate.' I felt sad as I said it. It's always sad when you break a link. I am not really a ruthless person although I must often seem so. Also, I felt just a little further away from reality with this step. Perhaps it had always been at the back of my mind that one day I *might* go back to him. But no, it wouldn't do. The marvel had been that he and I had ever come together in the first place.

'I'll see you are comfortable financially.'

I shook my head without speaking. I didn't want money unless I'd earned it, and I didn't want much of it even then. 'I can manage, thank you,' I said briefly.

'I'd like to think of you with some money,' he said irritably. 'I hate this way you have of living on a shoestring.'

'Yes, it is sordid, but it suits me.' I finished my coffee. 'Well, that's settled then.' I looked up. 'We needn't even meet again.'

'I can't just wash my hands of you. You're in trouble.'

I frowned. 'I think I am a bit. But it's nothing you can help with. I thought I'd made that clear.'

'I can pay for a lawyer.'

'It hasn't come to that yet. And anyway, in my job I have plenty of lawyers who would be ready to defend me. I'm in the martyrdom business.'

'I know you're your own worst enemy,' he said, half admiringly.

It wasn't quite true, although it was nice of him to say so; I was one or two other people's enemy as well.

'I'm too fond of you to want to be yours also,' I said. 'Go away and get yourself your nice divorce.'

We parted outside the restaurant. I wouldn't let him see me home. I could tell he was troubled: he held on to my hand when he said good-bye. 'I shan't do anything in a hurry,' he said. 'And don't forget to call on me if you want me.'

He wouldn't do anything about a divorce yet, I thought. If I wanted to hang on to him I could, I seemed to know the way. But it might be a rotten thing to do.

I was glad to be back home, even if only temporarily. Even people like me need a moment or two when they are at peace. I looked at my face in the mirror as I cleaned my teeth. There was a faint bruise beginning to show, which stretched up the side of my mouth towards my nose. Nothing more than a faint blue shadow at the moment: it was my first battle wound.

I looked at my watch. Still ten minutes before eleven. I let the minute hand move round to the hour before I picked up the telephone.

The telephone at the other end rang out but there was no answer. Once again I was patient and let it ring a full two minutes before I put it down. There were some cigarettes on the table by the phone and I considered smoking one, but why die young? I took several deep breaths instead and then I tried the same number again.

'Hello,' said Tony Tomlinson. 'Was it you before?'

'Who else?'

'I was just coming through the door when it stopped.'

'Any news for me?' I prompted him. 'From your friend the policeman.'

'Yes, I've had a word with him. The robbery took place in this division so he naturally knew a bit and he was willing to talk a bit about what he knew. It all seems straightforward. A car like yours was parked at the scene of the crime. One person, a woman, made a shot at getting the number and what she reports is close to the number of yours. It could all be coincidence. Apparently they are keeping an open mind.'

'I hope so,' I said.

'He thinks so, at all events. Your car is at present being examined with full scientific analysis and that ought to help clear things one way or another. So for what it's worth to you the answer I have come up with is that the police aren't bluffing. And the man who was shot has died.'

'And what part do they think I played in the robbery?'

'They are keeping an open mind about that, too. They know you were not actually present.'

'Do they know where I was?'

'Yes, they've checked with your sister.'

'Damn.' Eileen would have been alarmed and would have shown it. Also, she had a rash tongue and might have said anything. Even her manner of not saying anything might give the police ideas. She thought I was in trouble and hence would certainly reinforce any notion Detective Inspector Idden and Detective Sergeant Hodd might have already formed for themselves. Of course, she knew nothing.

'I really couldn't get any more.' Tony was apologetic. 'He was very cagey. He's always cautious, but this time he was really *piano*. You could read something into that if you liked, I suppose.'

Yes, you certainly could, but I didn't want to say so to Tony when he'd tried so hard. 'Thanks very much, you've done marvellously, Tony.'

'Keep in touch with me, will you? I might get more.'

'Oh?' That alerted me. It meant Tony was interested, and if he was interested then his extremely sensitive antennae were telling him that there was a big story coming. He might have got this from his policeman. Or, although I hoped not, he might have picked it up from me. 'I'll telephone occasionally then. But don't ring here, I might not be here very much.'

'Suits me. I'll send up smoke signals somehow if I want you,' he agreed amiably.

To calm myself I tidied the room a little. There was nothing in it I treasured or would mind leaving behind. It was better to live this way. There was only one thing in the three rooms which had any value for me.

I went to the table by the window. I used it to keep my make-up on: I won't call it a dressing-table. It had one drawer which I kept locked. I looked carefully at the drawer, automatically checking, but there was no sign that anyone had tried to force the lock. I supposed that the police might have ways to open the drawer without it showing if they wished, but I had seen no signs that the flat had been searched. It might be, some time in the future.

I opened the drawer and took out my diary. I am no Pepys (although like him, I write in my own secret cypher) and I never write at length. The historian of the future won't find a lot of interesting detail about my life in my diary.

I sat down, and after a moment's thought, wrote a few sentences. I rarely write more, but I felt a sort of compulsion to do so, as if the day which slipped away unrecorded had been cheated.

I had not written anything yesterday, the day of my meeting with Timothy, so that had been a day with which I had dealt fraudulently. I didn't mention Timothy. He had no place in this innocent and trivial account of the routine of my days. But he would lie at the back of it like the dark shadow of a secret illness. In other words, I would keep quiet about him.

I smiled and bit the end of my pencil. Then I tidied my diary away and went to get on my coat.

It was a pity to have to go out again, but I knew Timothy was expecting me. I didn't fancy a long walk, so this time I rang for a taxi and waited at the door for it to come. It was still well before midnight, and the city was brightly lit as always, but there were fewer people about to see the pretty lights and shop windows, and those that were about were moving more slowly, so that they seemed to be crawling along the darker stretches of the street. I've noticed this about evening street scenes. My taxi-driver was as surly as if a trip from one part of London to another was neither lucrative nor desirable.

I kept a watch out of the rear window. I'd had a nervous itch lately, as if I was being watched over. It didn't give me a feeling of protection either. I couldn't see any signs that I was being followed, but there was enough traffic around to make me unsure. Another car *did* follow me into Davenport Road, but it swept past as I got out.

I stood for a moment on the kerb, looking around, but all was quiet.

Timothy's part of the house was dark and still: he didn't come to my ring. Somehow I had imagined him answering it at once. I began to wonder if it had been a mistake to come. As I stood there in the dark doorway, waiting, I began to have an alternative picture of myself, going back to my place, packing a bag, taking up my passport, and flying from London airport that night. I had just enough money to get as far as New York if I wanted to go west or Athens or Istanbul if I wanted to go east. I could see myself flying out, wearing a belted rain-coat and an enigmatic look. I was the heroine of a Hitch-cock movie, or maybe I was the female crook: there often isn't much difference. I was going to be brought to the point of violence, come near seduction, be almost killed, but I would triumph in the end. The picture would end with my smile, half-triumphant, half-bitter (for naturally my experience of life had given me a taste of the sweet and sour). I had just got to the smile and my lips were beginning to take on an anticipatory curve when I heard the door open.

I stared for a moment out of the depths of my dream. 'I was miles away,' I said.

'How many miles?' he said, joining in at once.

'I was well beyond the Iron Curtain.'

'Were the spires of the Kremlin rising into view behind you?' he asked with sympathy.

'I don't think I was quite as far east as that,' I said doubtfully.

'In some unspecified country perhaps?'

'Yes, I think that's more like it.'

'I'm afraid that makes it a B film, probably,' he said. 'Vintage 1950.'

'That's exactly what I feel like now,' I said, walking through the door into the hall behind him. 'I felt definitely Hitchcock when I began, but you know how one can't sustain the imaginative effort.'

'There's only one Hitch,' he agreed, taking my coat. 'I mean, if we were every man his own Hitchcock, we wouldn't need to go and see the films, would we? Are you out of it now?' He stared in my face.

'Yes, I'm out of it now.'

I was back in London 1973, and standing in his flat in Davenport Road, but where that put me I wasn't quite sure.

'I am glad you came.'

'I said I would.' I took my coat from him and put it on a chair and then sat down myself.

'I wasn't counting on it. After all, why should you? I kept saying to myself: "Why should she come?" Once for curiosity, yes, but to come again you'd have to really like me and I wasn't sure you did.' He looked at me, trying to read some expression there which would give him a clue.

'I wasn't sure if you would be in,' I said.

'You know I won't be going out.'

I remembered the stores of tinned food, the signs of a careful provisioning, and related it to this remark. They fitted together like two pieces of a jigsaw, but they only made up a tiny piece of the picture, and I had plenty more of the puzzle to make out.

'You're under siege,' I said.

'Yes.' He came and sat down beside me. 'That's right.' He snapped his fingers. 'This is how it goes. I'm stuck here and I've lured you into coming here?'

'Lured?'

'Yes. You don't know that at first, but it gradually becomes clear to you.'

'Am I frightened then?'

'Oh yes, very, because you can see I might do anything. But you are only afraid at first; you are a girl of spirit and soon begin to think of ways of defending yourself.'

'That's good. I'm glad I'm a girl of spirit.'

'Yes, it makes it more amusing if you are a girl of spirit. No one wants to torment a girl with no spirit.'

I nodded. 'Oh, it's that sort of film. Is it very blue?'

'*No*. No, not at all.'

'Hammer, then?'

'No, I see it as more French intellectual. It *might* have a script by Marguerite Duras. Or be produced by Chabrol.'

I pursed my lips appraisingly. 'I begin to see it. How does it end? You can see I'd be interested in that.'

'I'm not sure.' He frowned. 'I don't see it yet. *You* end it, I think.'

There was dead silence. I was seeking for words when he got up and went to the cupboard. 'Let's have a drink.'

He gave me some white wine from an already opened bottle. I guessed he'd had quite a bit already. 'You're a very pretty girl, did you know that?'

'Oh, I'm an old hag.'

'You wear some rather awful clothes. That coat's all right; cashmere, isn't it? But what *have* you got on underneath it?'

'It's the sort of thing I wear to go out to dinner,' I said, squinting down at it. It was plain black jersey, rather long in the skirt, with a high neck.

'It's the wrong dress for you.'

'I don't take much notice about clothes,' I said. It wasn't quite true. I often had clothes fantasies in much the same way as, I suppose, people on a starvation diet have food fantasies. But whereas they dream of jam tarts, I dreamt of gleaming furs and fluttering chiffons and shoes from Gucci. But my life at the moment was not such as to consort well with elegance.

'I wish I knew more about you.' He came and sat down beside me again, glass in hand. 'I admire you so much, but I know nothing about you.'

'That's the whole point, isn't it?' I held my glass up to the light and admired the pretty colour. 'I'm a mystery to you and you're a mystery to me. That way we can tell stories to each other.'

'Do we tell stories to each other? Do I tell stories to you?'

'Oh, all the time.' I turned to look at him directly. 'Not still worried about killing yourself, are you? Remember telling me *that* story? The age fatal to genius and so on?'

'I remember.' He wasn't embarrassed. 'I wasn't telling you a lie. It just wasn't the whole story, that's all. Yesterday was my birthday. I did think of twenty-six as a kind of climacteric, but that was when I fancied myself a genius. And even then I only said to myself, "If you haven't achieved something by the time you are twenty-six you might as well be dead". I didn't promise myself quick extinction on the spot. I'm not quite a nut.'

'You sounded quite upset yesterday.'

'Yes, well, I've noticed that if you make that sort of remark it sometimes gets taken seriously and you find it's happening to you. I had a sort of superstitious dread of my birthday.'

I drank some wine. I accepted what he said. It sounded true enough. I might have felt the same way myself. He looked a bit younger than twenty-six, though. 'Are you sure yesterday was your birthday?'

52

'Yes.' He got up and went over to a small white painted desk, opened a drawer, and drew out a card.

I took it. On one side was a still-life of flowers and on the other side a message written in a large, round hand: 'Happy birthday, Timothy.' I sniffed it. It smelt very very faintly scented, as if it had been carried round in a woman's handbag next to her lipstick and her eyeshadow and her packet of cigarettes. 'From a woman?'

'Yes.' He took the card back and put it back in the desk.

'Well, lucky Timothy,' I said, 'to get such a nice card.' I drank some wine. 'I suppose you can't know her very well,' I said.

'Know who?'

'The woman who wrote the card. If you knew her really well she would say Dearest Timothy, or Darling Timothy, or nothing at all – just love.'

'She might be a very reserved girl,' he said.

'I believe she's your old maiden aunt.'

'I believe you're jealous.'

'No,' I said truthfully. 'Just trying to find out more.'

'About her or me?'

'About you both.'

He got up suddenly. 'I'll make some coffee. Put a record on the player. Let's have some music, something loud.'

The room had got considerably more untidy than when I had last studied it. Timothy had suddenly ceased to care for his possessions. A room which had given every indication of being constantly groomed now looked uncherished. This suggested a change of character. I was thoughtful. People under pressure do change, of course.

I took a short walk around the room. On the desk was some writing paper headed 'Archibald Press'. Tucked under the green blotter were a few unopened letters addressed to Timothy Dean, 4 Davenport Road. I put a Mahler Symphony on the record-player.

Timothy came in with some coffee. 'You don't open your letters,' I said.

'What?' He was occupied with arranging the cups on the tray.

I pointed to the unopened letters and he shrugged. 'Oh, bills only.' In fact, among them was one opened letter.

I took up this letter. 'I see you're thinking of moving.'

'What?' He looked startled.

I held it out. It was from a house agent, suggesting the price to be set on the flat and setting up arrangements for a sale.

'Oh that, just an idea I had.'

'I believe the reason you're hiding here is that you have accumulated a vast pile of debts and are hiding from the bailiffs,' I said idly, looking round the expensive and well-chosen furnishings of the room.

'Frank Capra comedy? Early depression?' he said alertly. 'Former millionaire, now broke, meets plucky little working girl. Did he ever use that theme?'

'No. We hadn't invented it for him then.'

'Pity.'

I stood up. 'Well, I never meant to stay long. I just thought I'd look in and check up on you.'

'Oh, don't go. Stay longer. Do please stay longer.'

'I think I won't, thank you,' I said deliberately.

He put his hand on my arm. I could feel the hard grip. 'You can't go.'

I stood quite still. 'You *are* mad,' I said.

'I need your company, I must have it.'

'Oh, go on, you can't keep me locked up.'

'Yes, I could, quite easily. I'm stronger than you are. I could tie you up, for instance, and gag you. I wouldn't do it, of course.'

'Well, thanks.'

'I want you walking and talking.'

What was it Lally had said? 'You attract all the nuts.'
I shook my head, half at myself and half at him. He saw
it and dropped his hand from my arm.

'I didn't mean it the way it sounded. You drive me to
an extreme way of talking. I only meant I want your
warmth, your support, your affection, if you've got any to
give.'

'I might have,' I said cautiously. 'What *is* wrong with
you?'

'Yes, I haven't been fair to you. I haven't told you a
straight story.' He walked away, threw himself into a chair
and motioned to the other for me. 'Sit down. I'll tell you.'

He had a way with him, you had to admit it. I had
intended to go, and here I still was, sitting listening to
him. 'Make it good,' I said.

'I told you I was in publishing? It means a fair amount
of travelling. Some of it outside this country.'

I watched his face. A muscle at the edge of his mouth
was twitching.

'Sometimes Europe. Sometimes the States.' He paused.
'So?'

'I meet all sorts of people. I talk to people, like them to
talk back. It's part of my job to encourage them.'

'Of course it is,' I said helpfully.

'On one of my trips to Amsterdam I met two men,
about my own age. We went to dinner at one of those
Indonesian restaurants that abound in Amsterdam, where
the waiters really come from Hong Kong. There are real
ones, of course, but I've never found one, there are so
many more of the others. I saw the two men next day at
London Airport. Chance, I thought ... I'd told them I
was going on to New York in a few days.' He stopped
again. He seemed to be having difficulty.

'Well, go on.'

'I was pleased to see them. I don't know why. I hadn't

55

liked them that much. They were just pleasant talkers to pass an evening with . . . I was lonely, I guess . . . We had a drink.'

'And one thing led to another, I suppose?' I said.

'That's about it.'

'And what did they have in store for you?'

'They asked me if I'd take some drugs into the States. The usual . . .' He looked down at his glass.

'And what did they offer you for doing it?'

'Quite a lot of money.' He swallowed again. 'I'm always hard up . . .'

I could believe him. He did look as if he had had money spent on him. Perhaps I mean he looked spoilt.

'I was to have half the money before and the other half after I'd done the job.'

'I wonder you weren't caught,' I said.

'I expect I would have been if I'd done it.'

'You didn't deliver the drugs at all?'

'No, I took the money and I dropped the parcel they'd given me in the Thames.'

'That *was* a good idea,' I said admiringly. 'It takes a genius to think of something like that.'

'I didn't believe they'd be able to do much about it . . . I didn't think they even knew my name.'

'And now you find they do know it?'

'I'm not sure what they know. But I have reason to think they're looking for me.'

'What sort of reason?'

He hesitated. 'I did take certain precautions, you know,' he said vaguely. 'I didn't tell them where I worked. I suppose they found out. I heard they were asking for me. Not by name, they don't know my name.'

'You *heard*?' I questioned.

'I telephoned. I can do a great deal of my work without going to the Press. I usually do.'

'That was one of your precautions, I suppose?' I said.

He didn't answer. 'I don't think they can hang around very long,' he said. 'They'll have to get back to Amsterdam.'

'What makes you think that?'

'I do think so.' He wasn't telling me everything, by any means. 'I think I only have to stay quiet for a bit and it will be all right.'

'Perhaps so,' I said slowly. 'You could always try. And what am I? Camouflage?'

'Something much nicer than that,' he said.

'What you are *really* telling me,' I said, 'is that you let two men down hard, and now they are after you?'

'I suppose so,' he agreed.

'I can understand that: I've often felt like doing some betraying myself.'

'You do say strange things,' he said uneasily. 'I never used the word betray.'

Was it after this I remember feeling hot and tired at the same time? I remember going into the kitchen for a drink of water. I felt sick. I heard a ring at the bell. I remember calling out to him, don't answer it. I don't know if he heard me. I think not, because he was calling out to me, and guess what, was calling the same thing to me. As usual, we cancelled each other out.

Was it after this that I came back into the room and found him dead? Is it possible that he really stiffened so soon into rigor mortis? And did the smell of decay come about so soon?

Chapter Three

'Say that again,' said the policeman. 'Tell that bit again. Come on now, you know the bit I mean, don't act stupid. You're not a stupid girl, not by any means. So tell it again. Begin where you went into the kitchen. Or rather just before that.'

'He said I was something much nicer than camouflage. Then I remember feeling hot and tired. Also sick.'

'What made you feel sick, Miss Cooper?'

'I . . . I don't know. I remember feeling hot and tired. And then I felt sick. Then I took a drink of water. I heard the front door-bell ring. It rings in the kitchen. He called out to me not to answer it . . .'

'Did you open it?'

'Yes. No one was there.'

'Did the bell ring again?'

'I believe it did. I'm confused. It rang later. This time a woman was there. She said something about noise. Strange how things move together. I remember drinking some water . . .'

'Go on, you drank some water, then what?'

'I drank some water, cleaned up. When I went back to the room I found him dead.'

'Are you sure he was dead?'

'He was stiff and dead.'

When she had been taken away, one policeman turned to the other.

'Well, what do you make of that?'

The other man was deliberate. 'She's not a liar. I'm sure she believes she's telling the truth.'

'How could she be?'

'Yes, that's right?' He picked up a cigarette. 'How could she be? The laws of physics would have to be contradicted.'

'Physics?'

'The thermodynamics of the body solids, the changed state of the body liquids as they cool. I suppose it's a form of physics? A physical law, anyway.' He lit the cigarette. 'How could a man be alive one minute and rigid dead the next?'

Chapter Four

In fact, after my drink of water, I believe I went back into the room. I had a story to tell him, too.

'I haven't been quite honest with you, either,' I said. 'Give me something strong to drink and I'll tell you. I'm frightened.'

'I thought you seemed uneasy.' He got up, went to the cupboard and produced another bottle. He held it up to the light. There wasn't much gin in it, but there was some. He must have been doing some drinking.

'If unease is all I show I've got a lot of self-control.'

'You've got a bruise on your face to go with it,' he said. 'What's up? In trouble?' There was a note in his voice different from any I had heard before. Coarser, somehow, as if trouble had joined us together and made the less of us both.

'First, I must go to the window and look out. May I?'

'Help yourself.' He waved a hand. 'It's something I do often, myself. All prisoners do.'

'Are you a prisoner, then?'

'Yes, a rather tiresome sort of prisoner. The sort that takes the key and locks himself in. No one likes *that* sort of prisoner. Prisoners ought to want to be free. It's expected of them. I wonder how many prisoners really want to, though, and aren't secretly frightened of the prospect. Freedom might be like death, mightn't it? Something totally unexpected.'

'Do you think death will be that?'

'It must be, mustn't it? Death, like God, must be unknowable.'

It was a pity God came into the picture just then with me rolling on my way to corruption. It troubled me rather.

'I told you about my car being stolen? And being used in a robbery and the police questioning me about it?'

'Yes, I remember every word. Wasn't it true?'

'True enough. I enquired around and found the police do have an armed robbery and a murder on their hands, and a car like mine was used. One very similar. They have a witness. They wonder if I am involved. You can't blame them.'

'I don't.'

'I think they are having me followed.'

'What makes you think that?'

'The usual thing. I keep seeing the same face.'

'Careless of them.'

'I think they want me to know,' I said. 'About being followed.'

'Could be.'

'Somehow I think they want to put pressure on me. They don't like me, you see. Nothing personal, they just don't like people like me.'

'You don't look to me like someone who robs a post office.'

'No, I'm not. But I tell you what, darling, I get the distinct impression they are after me for something.'

He looked at my face and then cocked his head on one side. 'Something you don't know about?'

'Well . . . could it be?'

'That would be *very* Hitchcock,' he said. 'The idea is that you just *feel* your way towards the crime, getting hints and then, wham, there's a body.'

'I don't like the sound of that.'

'Oh, it could be very intellectual, a Simenon-derived

plot, one in which you gradually begin to feel the burden of your guilt. That's known as the Find the Crime to Fit the Guilt plot.'

'Oh thanks, that sounds lovely. I shall enjoy being part of that one.'

'Have another drink before you jump out of the window and decide which one you're going for.'

'Can't you find me another plot?'

'Give me some more help then.' He leaned back comfortably and prepared to enjoy himself.

'Well, there's my husband.'

'Oh yes, that shadowy figure.'

'He's not shadowy at all.' Although I was critical of my husband I was quick to defend him from anyone else. I was ambivalent in my attitude to him, no doubt about it. In this, as in so much else, I was double-faced. 'But you say he can't possibly be concerned in the robbery.'

'Oh no, that's not my idea at all. But he has influential friends. I forget that sometimes. It's as well to remember. And he wants me to come back to him. He might have, I don't say he *has*, but he might have got them to be nasty to me so that I would be nice to him.'

'Could he do that?' He was rightly sceptical.

'He couldn't *invent* an occasion, but granted such an occasion exists, like this robbery, then he might be able to use it.'

'Seems a bit roundabout, and you don't seem quite the girl to respond to that kind of treatment.'

'I'm not.'

'No, it doesn't sound right. Plot has to begin with character, doesn't it?' He was more than a little drunk. 'And such detail as you have allowed me about your husband's character does not suggest that sort of behaviour.'

'No, it doesn't.'

'You might use that sort of strong line in a smart thirtyish gangster-cum-dirty-politics plot. Yes, it would work there. Veronica Lake, Alan Ladd; that style. Does he own a newspaper, your husband?'

'No. I think he may have put up the money for a small local one, though.' It had struck me that my husband was the possible source of the backing for Tony and David's news sheet. In which case it would not do to rely on them too heavily for support.

'That won't do, I'm afraid,' he said regretfully. 'Not big enough. Care to look out of the window now?'

He came across and joined me and we both stared out, pressed side by side together. 'Of course,' he said softly, 'we could make something very terrible and bitter out of it. Like something sombre and realistic, all photographed in sepia. Polish, perhaps. Anyway, the machine (no need to be specific, but perhaps in this case we might say the Police Machine) slowly and relentlessly reduces you to a nothingness.'

'I thought the vogue for that sort of film was over,' I said, with a shiver.

'The horrors are never *quite* over, are they? They always come back with a fresh face on.'

'Don't they, indeed.' What a lot he knew that I knew.

'Besides, you and I specialize in enjoying past gems of production. The hard, false *bijoux*. The essays in *kitsch*. The last theme I have outlined is hardly *kitsch*.'

Not *kitsch* enough, I thought. Not *kitsch* enough at all.

We stared out into the brightly lit street. Across the road an archway led into a private garage belonging to a block of flats. In the shadows a form could be seen standing.

'There's a man,' I said. 'I can see him.'

'And is he there for me or for you?'

'Hard to tell.'

'Who gave you that bruise?' he said softly. 'You didn't come by that for nothing at all.'

'A long while ago,' I said, 'I fell in love with the wrong sort of person and now he won't let me go. Keeps coming back.'

'Is he connected with the stolen car and the armed robbery?'

'He could be.'

'He's a criminal then?'

'By now, I think he is.'

'Is that the truth?'

'More or less. I'm leaving a bit out.'

'Then you are in trouble,' he said, and put his arm round me.

As we stood there a dark-coated figure passed slowly along the pavement on the other side of the road. He looked, or so I thought, unmistakably a policeman. The man standing in the archway retreated further into the shadows. He did not wish to be seen. It was then that I knew that I was being pursued, not by one group but by two.

Chapter Five

'So that's your story; an angry lover.' He nodded. 'It's a good one.'

'A very common one, I should think.'

Suddenly he said: 'Who are the heavies?'

'The what?'

'The villains, the opposition,' he explained impatiently. 'You have to have the heavies. In a western, for instance, they're usually the Indians. Not always, but usually. What are they in this case?'

'His friends, I suppose.'

'Really? What was he, your boy friend? A gangster?'

'You could say so.'

He said, 'Funny how your life and mine seem to run on similar lines.'

'Oh, we're on the same train?'

'*Are* we? Would you say so?' His eyes were bright. 'Somehow I sort of like that. Suits me, suits me fine.'

I had not told him that I had seen one man outside move quietly into the shadows, and a car slide silently into position on the kerb near the other. I wasn't sure if it was the police or not. It looked a pretty slick operation, so I guessed they were policemen. Or some of them were.

'And you've got to admit it's unusual.' He was smiling. 'Events don't normally fit into each other so neatly, do they? You know what, I think we're moving into a Patricia Highsmith plot.' He nodded seriously. 'One thing follows another, and you think, goodness that's clever. But life isn't clever. Or smooth. It's rough.'

I didn't tell him how rough I thought life could be, for me or for him. It wasn't the sort of thing you say to people; it's the sort of little discovery you leave them to find out.

'Go on about your lover,' he said. 'The one who had you beaten up.'

'How did you know he didn't do it himself?'

'I'm guessing,' he said dryly. 'You don't look like a girl who's had a love feast.'

'I was going to dinner with my husband. We do that sometimes. I think he wants a divorce. I'm not quite sure about that. I don't think he always tells me what's in his mind. He's uneasy about something. I hurried home to change. I went up the stairs. Two men followed me up. One held me while the other beat me.'

'Nasty.'

'It could have been much much worse. You see, they didn't hit me really hard.'

'I suppose your lover didn't want you broken into two. He must still desire you. Your ex-lover, that is. He *is* your ex-lover?'

There was a pause. 'More or less,' I said.

He counted up on his fingers. 'A husband, an ex-lover, more or less, me. That's three at least. What a girl you are.' He added, 'He sounds a tough, your ex-lover.'

'He believes in protecting his investment.'

'So it was a business arrangement?'

'Oh no, there was love involved,' I said wearily. 'In the beginning at any rate, and on my part.'

'And he's a criminal?'

'Yes, I think you'd have to call him that.'

'And you didn't know at the time?'

I shook my head. 'I didn't think about it.'

'No, you wouldn't,' he said thoughtfully. 'It would spoil the plot.'

'I'm telling you a true story.' To my surprise my voice came out fierce and strong. I sounded as though I really minded what he believed.

'Absolutely true? True in every detail.' He cocked his head at me. 'Yes, of course, an attractive girl like you would attract a good strong plot.'

'Please.' I was almost crying. 'Take me seriously. Take what I tell in earnest.'

'Oh, I do. A girl like you falls into trouble without looking for it.'

Outside in the street a man still stood who was a threat. Or two men.

I heard the bell ring once more. We looked at each other.

'Expecting anyone?' I asked.

'No.' His voice was grim. 'I'm not going to open it.'

I knew we had to; it was written into the script. If he did not, then I must.

'I'll go.'

I went to the door and opened it. There was no one. The hall was empty.

Afterwards, I was questioned at length about this episode, but I am sure this was how it was. No one was outside the door when I opened it. They say it cannot be, that it must have been at this point the killer came in.

'Who is it?' I heard Tim call out.

'No one.' I shut the door.

They say I shut the killer in but I say no, no, no, a thousand times no.

'What are you giggling at?' said Tim.

'I'm not giggling.' And indeed, I was not, all such giggles were a long time in the future or immensely in the past. I wonder now which he was hearing.

'You made a noise,' he said suspiciously, coming out of the sitting-room and staring at me.

'I caught my breath, it made me choke.' Choke, joke, giggle, you see how my mind was moving? It was a lie, of course, I hadn't made a sound. I said it only to placate him.

As who would not when death and violence hover? Between us two there must be amity.

'I'm certainly glad there was no one there. You can guess who I thought it might be?'

'Your drug-smugglers,' I said.

'Don't call them *my* drug-smugglers,' he said irritably.

'They're certainly not mine. I didn't invent them.'

'They exist all right.'

'Oh, I know they do. In 3D, too. No, it's the dialogue that worries me.'

'And what does that mean?'

'What language did they use? Was it Dutch? Or Turkish? Or even English?'

'They spoke English,' he said, after a pause. 'Naturally. I don't speak Dutch or Turkish.'

'No, I thought you didn't. Did you get the impression they were doing the talking themselves, or were the voices dubbed?'

'You can be quite vicious when you like,' he said.

'Not intentionally.'

'People always say that. But it can't be true, can it? We say what we really mean.' He sounded suddenly weary. 'Shut the door, will you? It's not quite closed.'

I gave the door a bang, so that he could hear it and be reassured.

I don't know what I let into the flat that day between the opening of the door and the shutting of it, but something terrible came in.

*

We were huddled together, he and I, like Eskimos in an igloo. Only our need was mental, we needed each other's support.

'Funny,' he said, 'that *both* of us should have people after us. You were looking for somewhere to hide and so was I.'

'And you've found it,' I said, my eyes going round the room.

'And so have you,' he said eagerly. 'Stay here. Stay with me.'

'I don't like the way you keep going back to that.' He made me uneasy. 'You know I can't. This place won't do for two.'

'Oh, it will. You've seen the preparations I've made. I could stand a siege. We'll stand it better together.'

'But I haven't got the siege mentality.' I felt an immense sadness. 'So I'm going.'

'But they'll kill you.'

'No, I don't think they will.' I was already getting my things together.

'Well, anyway, don't go until whoever is outside has gone away.'

'But there's no one. I looked.'

'Someone rang the bell,' he pointed out, reasonably enough.

'It was children playing a game.'

'At almost midnight?'

'City children play late.'

'And some games are very nasty.'

We eyed each other. We were close to quarrelling.

'You *know* it was not children playing ring and run,' he said accusingly. 'It's you who are playing games.'

'No, it wasn't children,' I admitted. 'And the bell did ring and we were not imagining it. Nor is this a ghost story.'

Then the bell rang again. A loud, insistent buzz.

'They're back.'

'Yes.' I was listening. I walked to the door and flung it open.

Outside was a tall elderly woman wearing a tweed coat.

'I came about the noise,' she said crossly. 'You're making too much. Please to stop it. I want to get to sleep even if you don't.'

Her appearance was so unexpected that I did not speak for a minute.

'The music,' she said, emphasising her words with little taps of her slippered foot. 'It's too loud. I live just above.'

'I'm sorry,' I stammered. 'I didn't notice.'

She gave me a contemptuous look. 'Try listening.'

'Was it you that rang before?'

'Don't try and make out that it's *me* that is the nuisance,' she said. 'I know your sort, but I know how to look after myself. I'll come in and turn down the noise myself if you don't.'

'No need.' I blocked her way.

'Well, remember, I'm just upstairs.'

'I'll remember.'

I watched her go up the stairs. At the turn of the stairs she looked back. 'Go on. Get on with it.'

I went back into the flat and closed the door behind me. Tim had disappeared. He was back in the living-room, sitting on a chair.

I went over and turned the record-player off. It hadn't really seemed so loud.

'I was listening,' he said. 'Where'd she come from? Outer space?'

'She seems to live upstairs.'

'Don't believe it. She came in on a green flying-saucer . . . I was peeping through the door and do you know what I thought?'

I looked at him. 'No.'

'I thought she had a gun in her right-hand pocket.'

'You're joking.'

'I'm not. I know a gun when I see one.'

'Well, perhaps. Oldish woman living on her own, she might be frightened.'

'She was *aggressive*.'

I had to admit he was right there. She had looked a fighter.

'*You* can be aggressive when you're frightened,' I said. 'I should know.'

'Are you frightened too?'

'I think I am. We're both in such trouble. And we're making it worse for each other.'

'Oh no. I feel safer with company.' He came very close and put his arms round me. There was a smell of cloves and sandalwood coming from his hair. I drew away.

'I'll have to go.'

'It's not safe for you either, outside,' he said, pressing me close. 'I mean if what you told me was true, about the demon lover. About the police, too.'

'Is what you told me true?'

We stared at each other, sceptically.

'You know, I think I've seen that old woman before,' he said thoughtfully.

'Of course. She lives upstairs.'

'I mean – *apart* from that,' he said absently.

'Oh great, now you're getting dreams about her.' I could just stop my voice showing irritation.

'In my position, you watch everything.' He was still staring back into the past, his eyes abstracted. 'I wish I could remember where I'd seen her.' He looked at me. 'She reminds me of someone, just a touch here and there.'

'Perhaps she's one of your drug-runners in drag,' I said flippantly.

71

He didn't react, and from that moment I ceased to believe in the drug-runners. It was a good try on his part, but it wouldn't do. I knew I had to leave.

'What a rotten time people in hiding have,' he said, suddenly. 'Cheap hotels, dreary flats over garages and hemmed in by shops. Always on edge. No way to live, but you could make a story.'

'It's been done often before,' I said dryly. 'Are you telling me you've lived like that?'

'Just imagining.'

I kissed his lips. 'I want to say good-bye,' I said.

It was a fatal kiss, fatal to him and fatal, no doubt, in the end to me. What I had not realized was that fear is a potent aphrodisiac. Who can know or find out? It's not the sort of thing they teach at school and you don't read about it in the pages of the women's magazines. It may make the medical journals, but even this I doubt.

'You know, the first time I came to see you here I didn't have any idea how I would really come to feel about you,' I said.

I remember kissing him and saying, 'I declare the war officially begun.'

It was at that moment we became lovers. Before we had only been chance companions and potential enemies.

After a while, I touched his bare shoulder and said: 'I've got to go and dress.' I don't think he answered me. I don't remember. I ought to remember but I find I do not.

I went to the mirror on the wall opposite to tidy my hair. I looked haggard and tired, which was not surprising. I saw nothing reflected in the mirror except my own image. No sign of movement, no hand, least of all a hand on a gun.

And yet, in another reel of the film, when I turned round he was already dead.

I would remember looking at him lying on the bed and seeing the red hole in his skull and thinking: 'It's not neat at all, that hole, in books they talk about a neat black hole in the skull, but this one is not neat, it's full of blood and hair and bone.'

Chapter Six

The police visited me early the next day and reported on my car. They had not yet returned it to me and showed no sign of doing so. I was still travelling on the tube or in a taxi. I wondered if I could charge my expenses to them.

They said the car had been used in the robbery raid; their tests gave decisive evidence. Of course, I knew they would say this. I even believed it was true. I expect the tests *were* positive. The police could have arranged for them to be positive. Just a touch here and a touch there, that's all you need to falsify. I *ought* to know.

I listened carefully. On such occasions it always pays to listen and not say much. Indeed, almost anything you say is probably going to be regretted later. Total silence is not advisable either (or even possible, the police see to that). There is a narrow path to be trod, and it has to be done delicately.

They told me more about the robbery. In fact, granted they were not men with much feeling for words, they gave me a pretty vivid picture of it. Two masked men, using my car (they did not hesitate to affirm it was my car), had entered a sub-post office, housed in a tobacconist's, had shot the postmaster in the head and then removed several hundred pounds. It was not luck, finding a relatively large sum of money: the postmaster was known to be casual about banking his takings. He had even been known to joke about it, which he would not do again.

They did not accuse me of being an accessory before the fact, but Detective Inspector Idden said he would show me a photograph of the two men and ask me if I could identify them.

I was surprised into speech. 'I thought you said they were masked.'

Idden smiled, a tight, unpleasing movement. 'The men we think they might have been,' he corrected himself.

'Oh, you have some idea, then?'

'Well, there are ways of guessing, you know. We don't start entirely from scratch.'

'No, indeed,' I said. A little bit of impertinence I might have restrained, because I saw his eyes give a nasty flick towards his Sergeant.

'For instance, we ask ourselves what men we know to be around at the moment who could stage that sort of job. Then we ask which of them has the *need* to do a job right now. These men don't work unless they have to.' He smiled at me. 'Of course, I call them men, but they could just as well be women.'

'You're not suggesting I'm running a league of women criminals?' I said tartly.

'I'm not suggesting anything. It's not my place to. I only put facts together.'

But I knew better than that. No one really just puts facts together, the human mind doesn't work that way, you have to start with an imaginary outline and fit the facts into it. The idea comes first, the facts come afterwards. Ask any scientist. The honest ones will agree and the dishonest ones will pretend they are detached observers. Detective Inspector Idden wasn't a scientist and probably not much of a thinker, but he knew how to go about getting evidence: you look for what you think is there. In this case, he had an imaginary picture of a crime and I was in it somewhere.

'Does the name Cruithin mean anything to you, madam?' he said.

'No, nothing.'

He terminated the interview there. I walked with them both to the door to let them out. His Sergeant had said nothing at all this time. I suppose he was saved up for special occasions.

At the door Idden turned. 'You don't mind if I talk to your husband?'

'We're not living together,' I said quickly.

He was too clever to say that he knew, but the very way he had put the question told me how much he had checked up on me. 'Could you give me his address?' he said politely. 'If you have it, that is.'

'Oh yes, I have it.' I wrote it on a piece of paper and handed it over. It's a good address. I hope it impressed him. But no doubt he knew it already and this question was just part of the game.

'Ah yes, that address,' he said, as if he knew another address for my husband which was different from this one. He put the piece of paper in a notebook and went away.

As soon as he had gone I telephoned my husband. He was a long while getting to the telephone, but then between him and me were a porter and a housekeeper neither of whom liked me, and both of whom knew my voice.

'Have you had a visit from the police about me?' I demanded. I thought they might have been there already. Some bit of inner knowledge was written on Idden's face.

My husband's voice came through to me rather faintly as if he was holding the receiver away from him. 'No, no visit.' I could hear noises in the background, as if he had someone there.

'Then you can expect one. They will be asking questions about me. Say what you like to them. Hold nothing back. I don't care.' Then I said, 'What's that noise going on?'

'The radio. I'll turn it down.' The noise stopped at once. It had been very faint, anyway. More like a voice talking than the radio. 'I'll answer any questions, of course, but you worry me. What am I supposed to say about you? Or not say?'

'I've told you I don't care. The police are convinced they can pin something on me and nothing you can say will make them think differently.'

'What have they got against you, Olivia?' he said earnestly. 'Be frank. I can get you a good lawyer.'

'They've been checking up on me. They know I work for an organization they doubtless don't approve of.' I hoped that was all they knew: it so happens there was more, but even as a front man for Shout I had been a trouble to them. 'They have my car and believe they can prove it was used in this robbery.'

'And *was* it used?'

'I don't know. I certainly hope not,' I said irritably. 'Not with my permission, anyway.'

'That is good news,' he said earnestly.

I scowled, but that did not come across the telephone line, although my frosty silence did. He broke it. 'Of course, I don't think of you as a criminal,' he said wearily. 'But you fall into trouble, and with your eyes open. Come back home, Olivia, and we will face the police together.'

'It's a good offer.'

'I can't quite cut you off, Olivia.' He sounded apologetic, as if loyalty and love were something even he could no longer put up a case for.

A bit of me wanted to cling to him, too, but I had gone too far. 'It will happen in time,' I said. 'Quite naturally, you'll see. You'll cut me off.'

'You sound sad.'

'Oh no, gay as a lark.'

'I'll stay around, Olivia.'

I was silent again. He had reduced me to apologetic silence too often and too easily in our life together: I suppose it was what did us in as a married pair.

'About your address,' I asked suddenly, remembering Detective Inspector Idden's knowing face. 'Have you now got *another* address? Are you moving somewhere else?'

When he answered it was in a different tone of voice, one I had never heard him use before. 'I have bought another house. But it was some time ago.'

'Will you be moving from where you are?'

'No, it's not certain. I'll let you know. It's all in the melting-pot.' Once again he sounded rejected and weary.

I was late now and knew I ought to hurry, or I would meet reproachful gazes from Sarah. She was a past mistress in the art of giving me such a look: she herself was exemplary, and never let her private life, if she had one, influence her standard of work. On occasions I thought she had no such private life at all and ceased to exist the minute she left the office; on other occasions I thought it might be very rich and full, providing her with that inner strength of which she undoubtedly had a great deal.

She had on her iron face that morning. It was never easy to be sure what that look portended, except that I would find the going hard. She had a little bag of integrity inside her. It was done up in the form of sharp, hard nails, and when she felt like it she distributed them around her pretty freely. She felt like it now.

She looked hard at the clock; I was late and I knew it. Now I knew that she knew it. 'Mr Fabyan's waiting,' she said.

'Oh yes, we were going to meet this morning.'

'That's right. He's got someone with him.'

'Oh, who?'

She shrugged. 'He said it was better if I didn't know.'

'Oh lord, not one of those again.' Fabyan (it was not his real name: I believe he was called Jenkins) was a professional conspirator. He was always turning up on my doorstep with a secretive look and a plot. Some of his plots were good, some bad, nearly all silly. He was always just about to produce a new, unpublished and hitherto secret testament by Solzhenitsyn. Or he could name the prisoner kept secretly in a dungeon in Brno. Or the man the Vatican most wished to silence. Sometimes I used to think he made all these tales up, other times I thought he must work for the C.I.A. But whatever he did, he wasn't straight and he wasn't nice. I always hoped that if I ever went to prison it wouldn't be him that was trying to get me out. But I expect it would be. I can't think who else would bother. Certainly not my husband. I should have worn out his love and charity long before.

I had a funny feeling at the thought of prison, as if I already knew it would be cold and bad and I would not like it very much, but it would be better than my kind of death, because my kind of death would be absolute and without hope of salvation.

He came in, accompanied by a thin little girl wearing big spectacles. 'We're in business.' He didn't wait for me to speak, but put his arm round the thin girl and said: 'This is the girl we have to help, her and her sisters.'

'How many sisters?'

'No sisters.' The girl shook her head; she had a husky deep voice which sounded too big for her.

'I didn't mean it literally.' He butted his bushy Afro hair-cut at me. 'I mean all the girls on their own like her, the girls on their own with a child. It's hard for them to find a place to live. Ask her, she'll tell you. It's rough.'

79

'Very hard,' she agreed, in that deep, hoarse voice.

'Now we've got to take up their cause, make an issue of it.'

I thought she looked at him cynically, as if she'd been a cause or an issue before, and knew the ropes and thought nothing of it.

'I've got a whole file of cases like yours,' I said to her. 'Some I've helped, others I haven't helped.'

'Cases!' He was practically spitting at me. 'They're people.'

I fixed him with my special, opaque, businesswoman's stare which I keep for such occasions. It was closely related to the stare the Gorgon used. I've got Gorgon-blood myself, of course, it goes way back on the distaff side.

He told me the story I had known he would, full of all the details I could have provided myself: hostility, lack of money, isolation. I knew it all.

'Where do you live now?' I said to the girl.

She muttered, 'Near Swiss Cottage.'

'I can put you in touch with a friend of mine. Two friends, in fact. They are starting a news sheet to take up troubles like yours.' I could do two good turns at once. Perhaps help her and at the same time give David and Tony a leading story. 'I'll give you their address.' I pulled a pad of paper towards me.

After they had gone Sarah came into the room. I suppose no one had ever called her Sally, still less Sal.

'Telephone call,' she said. I knew who it was, from the very special note in her voice. It held reproof, yet admiration too.

'Hello, Lal,' I said. 'What's up with you?'

'I ought to ask you that.' She sounded as though she had smoked a great many cigarettes since breakfast, gone to bed very late the night before, and generally beaten herself up. Of course, Lal very often did sound like that, because that was the way she lived. 'I wish I'd never borrowed your car. I seem to have been on the police's visiting-list ever since.'

'You're not the only one.'

'I'm sorry it got pinched, Olivia, I really am.'

'It wasn't your fault,' I said wearily. 'What did the police want?'

'Just talk. I don't like their faces. What *were* you doing when the robbery was happening?'

I sat very still. I could feel my hand gripping the telephone hard. This was the first time someone had actually come out and asked me that in so many words, although the police had nibbled at the point with their questions about my sister and my visit to her. And now it had to be Lally asking.

'I was with my sister, I expect,' I said.

'You *expect*?'

I pointed out: 'I don't happen to know exactly when the robbery took place.'

'Just when he was closing the shop. Six-thirty, on Saturday. Where were you then?'

'Six-thirty? Now let me think. I know, I took my sister out for a meal. I thought she needed a rest. We often go to an Indian restaurant near where she lives. She likes spicy food when she's pregnant. Yes, we went to the Taj Mahal.'

'What did you do with the children?' said Lally; she was always passionately interested in this kind of detail in people's lives.

'We left them with my sister's husband.'

'I love the way you put that,' said Lally. 'It shows something about you, I think. Most people would say: we left them with their father.' Then she said: 'Still, that isn't all

81

I rang about. I wanted to tell you something about myself.'
She paused.

'What is it, Lally?'

'I'm leaving the boutique.' I was surprised. Surrounded
by the clothes she loved, but never wore, able to live in a
muddle there and not be scolded, for Lally it had seemed
ideal.

'But I thought you adored it there.'

'Yes, I do. But it isn't a life's work. Besides, Hertz is
selling it. I have to move on, anyway.' She spoke with the
calm understanding of one who had been 'moved on' by
more than one exasperated employer. Not everyone could
stand Lally's dreaminess and unpunctuality, even if what
they got in exchange was charm, honesty (of a sort) and
unbroken good humour. Mrs Hertz of Parade had seemed
to be one who could. Largely, I thought, because her own
life was extremely involved: she was probably glad to
meet someone as muddled as she was. The Lallys of this
world have an instinct for seeking out their kind. It was
no accident that Lally and I were best friends.

'What will you do? I wonder if I can help?'

'Oh, no, thank you,' said Lally hastily. 'Better leave me
to sink or swim on my own. I shall, anyway.'

This was true. Lally neither gave advice nor took it. It
left her wonderfully free. She owed no one anything.
Sometimes a little money, but in Lally's world that hardly
counted.

As you will have seen, sometimes it did count in mine.
I had a keener eye than my friend for material values.
But I was just as likely to die poor as she was.

'So you want to see me, Lally?' She was still hanging
on to the telephone, making heavy weather of the conversation, as if she still had something to say to me, but
did not know how to say it.

'Oh no.' She was clear about that, anyway. I suppose

she still had a guilty conscience about the theft of the car, although guilt and Lally were usually very very far apart. Then she went on: 'You know that diary you just sent me and asked me to hide for you?'

'Not *hide*. Just keep safe for a time.'

'Yes, that was it, to keep safe.' Her voice was sagging. 'Well, I can't find it.'

'You mean you've lost it?'

'Not lost, just mislaid.'

'I'll come round and help you find it,' I said savagely.

'It wasn't important, was it?' she pleaded.

I didn't answer. 'Not important, Lal,' I said at last. 'Just personal and private.'

I couldn't help wondering why she had chosen to tell me now, but she had told me and I would have to do something about it. 'I'll come round tonight, Lally, and help you look. We'll look together.'

'Oh yes, we could do that,' said Lally, but she didn't sound hopeful that we would find anything. My car and my diary in the space of a few days: Lally had had quite a losing spell.

I had one other errand before I could face Sarah again. I telephoned my sister. Like me she hates the telephone; it is one of the few things we have in common. 'Hello,' she said reluctantly, as if she had woken from a deep sleep.

'Hello, Eileen. I wanted to talk to you about last Saturday, and what we did.'

'I didn't see you till Sunday, remember,' she pointed out, thus proving she was not asleep. 'You turned up on Sunday morning.'

'If anyone asks, say we were out together on Saturday evening, eating at the Taj Mahal.'

'All right,' said Eileen indifferently. 'Where were you really?'

I hesitated. 'I had to go to a meeting,' I said.

'Oh? It's a pity about the Taj Mahal,' said Eileen.

'Why? It's not closed or burnt down, is it?'

'No, but it gives me terrible indigestion when I eat there. Where was your meeting?'

I was very, very still. 'In hospital,' I said.

'That's a good idea,' said Eileen. 'And long may he stay there.'

I think she must have heard me swearing because she at once broke the connection. Eileen hates anyone to swear. She says her husband never does, or at least not in her hearing.

I knew I wouldn't have long to wait for the next move from the police; I could almost have predicted what they would do and I was almost pleased when it happened.

Almost as soon as I'd finished talking to my sister, the police were on the line. It was very good timing, really.

'Sorry to bother you again.' It was Hodd speaking, a smooth pig. He wasn't sorry, he was glad, he was doing it on purpose. It was an impertinence to apologize. He and I both knew that apology was not in his mind. 'Just something I should have asked before.' He'd hardly opened his mouth at the interview; his superior had done all the talking. 'This is it: you were staying with your sister the week-end of the robbery? Right?'

'Right,' I said sourly.

'What did you do, did you do anything special? Go out or have people in?'

'We went out.' He could drag it out, word by solid word.

'Where did you go?'

'Out to dinner.'

'And you remember where?'

'Of course I remember where: an Indian restaurant, the Taj Mahal. I don't suppose you know it. It's in Lulworth Road, near my sister's home. Opposite the tube station, in fact. I don't suppose they'll remember us eating there, but my sister will, of course. She'll tell you. I'd rather you didn't bother her, though. She gets very fussed these days.'

'So you just had a quiet evening together?'

'Yes.'

There our conversation ended. Sooner or later the Sergeant would check with my sister, who would repeat what I had asked her to say, and sooner or later my sister would do some checking on her own account.

Unluckily she knew who to check with, so this called for some action on my part.

Chapter Seven

I did the most sensible thing I could in the circumstances. I went to see my brother-in-law who is (so interlocked is our family) also my cousin. He doesn't like me a lot, for which I don't blame him. I don't like him too much, either. I knew what he held against me, but he wasn't quite sure what I disliked about him, which gave me a slight advantage. He experienced a generalized discomfort in my presence, like having a short temporary illness. It puzzled him; he didn't recognize it for the waves of silent criticism coming from me. He didn't know what it was that troubled him, but he had enough sense of self-preservation to keep away from me as much as possible.

'Hello,' I said. 'Can I push in?'

'Oh, Olivia.' He stood up behind his desk. He had nice manners! It wasn't *that* I had against him. 'You don't often visit me.' My brother-in-law owns a small timber-yard, specializing in high-quality wood. So his office is always full of the smell of new wood and the furniture is dimmed with a layer of fine sawdust. You can usually write your name on his desk. From outside came the whine of a circular saw and the shouts and bustle of men shifting timber. As a place it both depresses and frightens me.

'Not often,' I agreed.

We stood looking at each other. Clouds of distrust floated above our heads like cigarette smoke. You could almost see it thickening in the air.

'Have a cigarette?' said my brother-in-law. He looked about him as if he might see a box of them. 'I know I *did* have some somewhere.'

'Not now.'

My brother-in-law had never forgiven me for conceiving a child when unmarried; my sister never forgave me for causing her to be adopted. And I never forgave myself for anything.

There were two men waiting for me outside the church the day of the funeral. Perhaps they knew I should be at my very weakest then. They recruited me and for five years I lay idle, a sleeper, unused. But they were gifted with precognition and knew my day would come.

'Mrs Devlin,' one said, coming forward and holding out a hand. 'We were told to contact you. We followed you here.' The coffin came out then and both men crossed themselves. 'What we want at the moment is an address. Somewhere to stay. Just for a night or two.'

An easy suggestion for starters to the main meal. But they were to continue eating. In fact, I was about to take a banquet, although a delayed one.

I recall saying: 'How did you know where to find me?' And one of them smiled and answered in a thick accent, 'But you're a famous lady.' I took them to an address I knew, an old lodging-house near Euston Station, and left them there. Years ago now, but I had reason to believe the lodging-house was still in use by similar men.

'Sit down, then.' He drew up a chair. 'What is it?'

'I've told Eileen a lie. And I want you to stop her finding out.'

He looked at me even more doubtfully than he had been doing. It was unlucky for him that I could always read his thoughts so well, although my sister, and this was perhaps

87

lucky for her, apparently could not. Now I knew he was thinking: Olivia is really very like Eileen in looks. You'd know they were sisters. Thank God I'm not married to her.

'Well, I expect you've told her other lies in the past,' he said.

'Yes, of course. And so have you.'

He flushed. 'I think I *will* have that cigarette.' He dug around in his desk and finally found a battered packet of ten. They looked unappetizing, but he took one and lit it. I felt sorry that the sight of me had driven him to such a relic.

'I don't want her worried,' I said.

'She's worried already about you, and, looking at you now, I'm not surprised. You look terrible.'

I took out a mirror from my handbag and had a look. He was right: I looked strained and anxious, worse than I felt, really. Reflected in my mirror I could see the book-case placed against the wall behind me and to the left of that a dark green filing-cabinet. I was beginning to dislike mirrors.

'Yes, that's a bad way to look,' I said. I put the mirror away, I didn't like looking at my face in the mirror. It reminded me of something. I didn't know what.

Perhaps it was the room giving me bad thoughts.

My brother-in-law's office was as uncompromising and austere as I remembered it, and the furniture as ugly. I had been here perhaps three times in the years he had been married to my sister, and always at times of crisis, either for him or for me. No wonder he was tense.

'You should take care of your appearance,' he said, almost angrily. 'You'll be a hag before you're thirty.' I could read his thoughts again. This time he was thinking: I wish she'd leave me and Eileen alone. She's bad for Eileen. 'Tell me what it is you want.'

Very briefly, I told him about my car being stolen, and how the police suspected me of being involved.

'I asked Eileen to tell the police I was with her when I wasn't.'

'You can take that request back for a start,' he said angrily. 'I won't have you involving Eileen in anything.'

'Yes, that's all right. She can tell them the truth. Say I wasn't with her, say what she likes. I can think up something to explain it to the police.

'They knew it was a lie anyway, I could see it written on their faces. Only I told Eileen *another* lie. I told her I was at a meeting. She thinks she knows with whom. I don't want her checking with that person, it could be dangerous. I want you to stop her. You are her husband, you ought to be able to do it.'

'I suppose I can stop Eileen doing some things. Not everything, though. She's too much like you.'

'You can stop her doing this. She'll take advice. And she's not well. I just don't want her going to talk to this person to find out if that's where I was when I pretended to be with her.'

'Ever since I've known you, you've been in this trouble and you've been in that trouble, almost all of it your own doing, but the funny thing is I've always respected you. I've always thought of you as someone who did what had to be done.'

'Yes, that's me,' I said sadly. 'And I've done it once too often. Speak to Eileen for me, will you? Forbid her to go probing around. Make it an order. She's old-fashioned about marriage, she might just obey.'

'She'd do it because she loved me,' he said, looking at me with defiance. And he might very well have been right. But the sad thing (and it was one of the strikes I had against him) was that he had no idea what her love was compounded of, how it had affection in it, and humour and protectiveness and an infinite tenderness. I've seen it and thought it was wasted on him. Any common or garden love would have done for him.

'And because she loves you,' he went on. 'But you don't deserve it, and you don't understand it, though you get the benefit of it.'

Say what you like, there was sympathy of a sort between my brother-in-law and me. Ideas bounced backwards and forwards between us. Whether we liked it or not, we often seemed to echo each other's thoughts.

'I had a good reason for lying to her,' I said. 'I was with a man. I didn't want her to know.'

'She seems to have guessed that, anyway. Do you think she would have been shocked?' His tone was cold.

'I wouldn't have said anything to you now if I hadn't needed your help. Keep Eileen out,' I said.

'And what's so special about this one? Is he a criminal?'

It was quite difficult to lie to my brother-in-law when he gazed straight at you. He looked kinder and yet more astringent than I had ever seen him. 'He's an associate of criminals,' I said reluctantly.

'And the *other* one,' he pressed. 'The one Eileen thinks you did spend the time with? The one she's going to talk to? Who is he? I have a right to ask? You agree I have a right to ask?'

'He's someone we both knew years ago when we were young.'

'I see.' He was staring hard now.

'There's no need to jump to any wrong conclusions.'

'Of course not,' he said stiffly.

'It's no one Eileen was very fond of, I can tell you that.'

'I quite understand.' Eileen said that he wasn't jealous, but he would really prefer to believe that she had had no previous existence in any form until the moment he

90

laid eyes on her. I dare say there are a lot of men like that, only my brother-in-law is an advanced example.

'He's a mad one,' I said. I suppose something crept into my voice that coloured it.

'Well, you've answered one question, anyway. *You* liked him.'

'I don't want Eileen doing anything about it. I want her to leave me alone.'

'Because it's dangerous?' he said sceptically, showing to me then that he didn't really know anything, his world was too sheltered.

'I haven't been quite open with you,' I said. 'I said it was dangerous. So it is. It's dangerous for me.'

Through the open window came the scream of the saw as it sliced at a chunk of wood, severing the vegetable matter, tough and hard, with a shriek. It got into my head, so that I began to ask myself if it was the wood or the metal saw that screamed. How can we be sure?

My brother-in-law got up and closed the window. 'Sorry about the noise. I hardly hear it myself. You get used to it.'

I picked up my bag. 'You'll do what I ask?'

He nodded. Again my eyes were caught by the large mirror on the wall and I could see my face reflected in it. The image seemed to waver and change. I suppose there was a flaw in the mirror. 'It seems to me that what you need is a lawyer,' he said. 'Do you want me to get you one?'

I paused at the door. 'That's a good idea. I know how to get one, though, if I need one. The organization I work for has one. He'd help me.' The lawyer was a tough, silent man who would certainly give me good advice, but I knew the advice would be grim. I guessed that it might be impossible to help me.

Suddenly I saw that this was really why I had come to my brother-in-law's office. Not for myself but because I

91

wanted Eileen and him to have a chance to get clear away from me, they really deserved it.

'Are you all right?' said my brother-in-law. 'You've gone quite white.'

'I feel quite well,' I said with honesty. 'I'm just a little frightened, that's all. You can understand that, I expect?'

'You're a funny girl.' A note of wry sympathy had crept into his voice. Now I was going, he could feel sorry for me.

'I'm going to take me and my troubles off your shoulders,' I said. 'I'll say good-bye.'

'Well not for ever, I hope.' He was trying to speak lightly. 'Don't make it sound so final. You haven't been condemned to death.'

See? He *could* read my mind, my brother-in-law.

So that was it. I was out in the street again and it had turned into a hot London day. I have loved such days, felt happy and free, enjoyed the smell of dust and diesel oil, but not now. It reminded me of frying oil and the tortures of the Inquisition and the ceremony of the *auto da fé*. When I had looked at my face in the mirror, I had seen a face already damned.

At the street corner I stopped and bought a paper from a news-stand, more for something to do than because I wanted to read it. I felt I already knew all the news there could be that day, and it was all bad.

I looked through the paper as I walked along on my way. But within it there was nothing there to interest me. I recall feeling puzzled. And I was puzzled that I was puzzled. And puzzled that I was puzzled that I was puzzled.

I had to check my thoughts, they led to bewilderment. I went into the office. Sarah was there as usual, looking like order personified. She had deep blue shadows under her eyes, however, so perhaps order was not achieved without strain. She was sorting letters, and looked at me bleakly before returning to her work.

'I know.' I went to my desk. 'I'm late again.'

'I put your personal letters on your desk,' she said.

There was only one letter, this was her own way of showing anger. Sarah could be devious. Or was that the right word? For the first time I spared the time to look straight at her, and see her as a person. It was almost too late for me to look at Sarah, but I did so. I saw a troubled, anxious girl who didn't want to meet my eyes.

I stared at my letter. If it had been anyone else but Sarah, I would have said she had been crying. But it was an axiom of my life that Sarah did not cry, that Sarah was without emotion. Of course, it had always been a game I played to myself. But for me it had undoubtedly been a convenient game. It enabled me not to worry about Sarah. Otherwise I might have had to because she was a charming girl, the sort to create affection even in someone like me. My game was wearing thin now.

My letter was handwritten; it was from my husband, and I was disquieted to see it. I knew I would have to read it. I folded it into a tight wad and put it into my bag. I didn't look at Sarah, but I was well aware that she was watching me under her lashes.

The morning went on quietly. I was relieved to have to work hard at matters demanding concentrated attention. I was glad when a hysterical young mother forced her way into the office to confront me and Sarah and we were forced to join together in order to calm her and give her a cup of hot, sweet tea. I was glad when the kettle boiled over on to the floor with a loud spurt.

'Phew,' said Sarah when we'd finished and she was tidying up. 'Poor kid. She ought to shoot that husband of hers.'

I didn't answer. Shooting your husband is easier said

than done. You need a gun to begin with and you need nerve. The nerve you need is surprising. That's what really shook Lady Macbeth, not the blood. She was a country girl, she knew all about blood and death, but what she didn't know was how hard it can be to kill. And she was after a crown. Some stake.

How much more courage is needed to shoot yourself? I drew open the bottom drawer of my desk. Inside was a gun. I closed the drawer. Sarah had not seen. She was far away in her own world.

When I was young and lived with Eileen and my other brothers and sisters deep in the country, we had a local lane jocularly called Sweethearts' Lane, and we used to say we could tell the girls who had been for a walk down Sweethearts' Lane by the look in their eyes. We didn't mean too well by this remark, as you may have guessed. Sarah looked to me as though she had been for a walk down Sweethearts' Lane. Several long walks. I wondered why I hadn't thought of it before.

The telephone rang and I knew without telling it was for me. Silently Sarah handed it over to me.

'Olivia? You know that diary that you hid with me . . .?'

'Left, Lally, left.'

'Left, then. It got lost, remember? It's turned up again.' She didn't sound triumphant or even pleased.

I looked across at Sarah, she wore an aloof expression as if I wasn't in the room at all. 'What are you getting at, Lally?' I asked.

'I think it's been studied, read. Someone's had it. It looks different and smells different, not of me, not of you. You know what a nose I've got.' Lally knew the names of a hundred different scents and could tell by smell who had passed down a passage before her. 'The last person in contact with your diary, Olivia, smelt of sweat and cigarette smoke. A man, I expect.'

'Whom the gods wish to destroy they first drive mad,' I said absently.

'You're not an ancient Greek,' said Lally, recognizing a quotation.

'No, alas.'

'Doesn't seem your life style, somehow,' said Lally sceptically.

'I only meant if I had been an ancient Greek I'd have been dead for several thousand years.'

'God, you *are* in a bad state.'

I kept quiet. A beat of time passed. I was still alone.

'Are you there?' asked Lally anxiously.

'Yes, I'm here.'

'Is it what I said? About someone having read your diary? It's true, you know. But is it that?'

'What do you think?'

I heard her take a little sucked-in breath. 'Oh, why does it matter so much?'

I could have said: It's got my life in it, that's why, and someone cares enough or is curious enough to want to read it. Instead, I said: 'Perhaps it doesn't matter, Lally. It's just one more perplexing thing. And you may be wrong.' But she wasn't wrong, I was sure. Some things Lally got terribly wrong; me, for instance, I wasn't at all what she thought me, but not this. On this she was right.

I heard her say she was sorry, and it sounded as if she was crying. I did just wonder why Lally was crying for me.

I knew from past experience that Lally only cried if she was angry or if she felt guilty.

There was one more interruption to my morning's work. Just before we broke for lunch I heard feet on the landing outside. We're right on the top floor and the eighteenth-century floorboards are bare. You can hear

95

every arrival and up here, the end of the climb, we know it's traffic for us.

Sarah raised her head and listened for a second, then bent her head stiffly over her typewriter. She looked all wrong this morning; usually she was such a graceful girl.

I was still thinking about Lally's message on the telephone. Behind that I was deeply preoccupied with worry about my sister. The door opened with a jerk that shook its delicate aged timber.

Bert Palmer, the caretaker, who lived in the basement, was standing there, holding out to me a long slim box. 'These flowers come for you. Just left at the door they were, so I brought them up.' He paused hopefully, on the lookout, as ever, for a piece of gossip, a bit of information to relish and then pass on, a bit digested, but still quite eatable. 'You getting married or something? Or buried maybe?'

A blow like a hammer hit me just above the heart. That was it, I thought, looking at the flowers, that was more like it. The long white flowers were chrysanthemums, flowers for a funeral. It was me that was dead, not Timothy Dean.

I felt sick. Then blackness crept up on the edges of what I could see and sounds receded. I could see that Sarah was standing up and saying something, but I could not hear. Then the blackness crept over my eyes.

I was resting on something hard, and there seemed to be a cover over me. It was soft and light and smelt of verbena. I knew without being told that it was Sarah's tweed coat. I looked up at the ceiling and recognized a familiar stain where the snow had come in last year. I was lying on the floor of my office. There was something rolled up under my head. I turned to look. It was my own coat, turned into a makeshift pillow.

I didn't faint, I thought, I merely absented myself from the world for a little. And who could blame me? I closed my eyes for a minute.

I could hear Sarah's voice. She was in the next room, but she must have had the door slightly open. She was talking to someone. I had joined her in the middle of a sentence.

'Looked awful ... late ... white,' I heard her say. She was keeping her voice low, so that I missed a word here and there, but I could easily fill in the gaps. She had a note in her voice I had never heard before. I lay there, eyes closed, and assessed it. She's talking to someone she knows very well, I thought, and someone she likes.

'I'm glad you came,' said Sarah. Someone she loves, I thought.

I turned comfortably on my elbow to listen: I was still a little way out of the world. Then I stiffened.

'I wrote yesterday telling her I would be coming now. Did she mention it?'

It was my husband's voice. And I heard Sarah making a low response.

And then him again. 'I can't just abandon her; she's so lost. I can hardly bear to look at her.' That was *me* he was talking about. I was outraged. I raised myself to listen further.

Sarah murmured something quiet.

'Just once more,' I heard my husband say. 'I must just try once more. You of all people ought to understand.'

'Yes, I'm dedicated to looking after the lost, aren't I?' said Sarah with quiet bitterness. Her voice had risen. Women always give themselves away at moments of exasperation by raising their voice. Either this is a general truth or I have had the luck to be married twice to men who can keep their voices down. I knew so much about Sarah now that I was shocked I could have been oblivious to it for so long. No wonder Sarah had been up when I was down and down when I was up. Her life and mine were indeed linked. I was back to my philosophical concept, and I could see truly that my little egocentric unit was interlocking with hers like a cogwheel. We were bound to pull each other round, probably for all eternity. That was another philosophical concept and not one I relished. There's a lot of space in eternity, and more than a suggestion of loneliness.

'My dear,' said my husband. 'Dear darling Sarah, it'll come out in the end, I promise you, but I must look after Olivia for a little while longer. I have to try.'

Poor thing, I thought, he still believes in a happy ending.

'I'll give it you, then,' I said. 'It's the last, the only present. I'll give you a happy ending.'

Although I hadn't really spoken loudly, I suppose they must have heard a noise because Sarah came in and knelt down beside me. 'Better?'

'I wasn't really ill,' I said. 'It's all a matter of blood sugar. I forgot to eat breakfast.' My throat felt tight and I licked my lips. 'I'd love a drink, I'm so thirsty.' I didn't mean to sound pathetic, but I must have done so because Sarah's face stiffened and I could see she was back to disliking me again.

While she was out of the room I got up and sat at my desk. Slowly I tidied myself up. My hand shook a little and I avoided looking in the mirror, but otherwise I was all right. While I was waiting for Sarah to come back I took my husband's letter out and looked at the envelope. I wondered if it would ever be necessary for me to open it. The envelope was creased and grubby from its stay in my handbag. I put my hand on it as if I might read its contents through the palm of my hand and be spared the pain of actual vision. Always until now I had had at the back of my mind the thought that, in the end, if I really wanted to, I could take up again my life with my husband. It was my little unacknowledged reserve of property. Now it no longer was mine. Sarah had pre-empted it.

I could hear the kettle begin its familiar scream as it came to the boil. In a second Sarah and my husband would be in the room with me, bringing a nice, hot cup of tea.

I didn't wait for the tea. I don't know now how I travelled. Afterwards the police asked me about this, but I had to answer that I did not remember. I know I travelled through a timeless day. The light seemed to belong to neither noon nor dusk. I don't know where the light came from, I remember no shadows. But I have a clear picture of myself sitting at my desk listening to the kettle boil and coming to a decision.

I got up, put my coat round my shoulders and quietly went out of the room.

Across London a telephone rang in a police station. It was a small station in a quiet district where life was sleepy and the man at the end of the telephone was surprised to find himself receiving a call. That was unusual.

'Hello, would you say that again?' he said sharply.

'I want to report a murder,' said the caller slowly, even hesitantly. 'There is a man lying dead.'

The voice stopped.

'How do you know it's murder, madam?' said the policeman.

'Shot,' said the caller thickly. 'Through the heart. Through the middle of the heart. It was through the heart and through the brain simultaneously. Fire at one and you kill the other. Make what you may of that.'

It was at this moment that the police constable experienced the first stirrings of doubt. 'What's that you said? Where is this murder? Can you give me the address?'

'Care of the heart,' said the voice. Then there was silence.

The policeman recorded all the details of this conversation together with the time and the date 10.40 hours, Wednesday, 10 October 1973. Underneath he scrawled for his own benefit and in pencil (he would erase it later): 'A bloody canary.'

Canaries are women that sing to the police and the note of hysteria in the voice is what makes them yellow canaries.

Chapter Eight

I must have made an interesting picture as I hurried away. I'm glad I was spared the sight. I'd like to hang on to what dignity I have left; in my own way I take myself seriously, you must have noticed, and I doubt if that small figure hurrying through the streets had much dignity. I was small because I had shrunk. I began shrinking the day I met Timothy Dean and there wasn't much of me left by now. A little bit of the vital body liquids dried out each day; my bones were turning into liquid calcium and draining out through my kidneys like tooth-paste; my blood was thickening and the vital minerals burning away. I had projected myself into space and must take the consequences.

With weightlessness went timelessness as a natural companion. I could not tell the time of day. But I had been used to this lack, to tell the truth, for some while now. It had been growing on me. The clock which we all keep inside us had checked and was now faltering to a stop.

I remember crossing the road against the light and having a taxi-driver swear at me. I recall passing a telephone-box, and then standing outside a church at the corner of a busy main road. It was a dark, dusty Victorian building which I must have seen often before, but now seemed to see for the first time. I stood looking at it, wondering if I could go in. Churches are said to be sanctuaries of prayer and refuge, but I have noticed that they are not particularly welcoming places in spite of this tradition. Some seem actually to dislike being disturbed in the contemplation of their brasses and monuments. This church might not be like that. I should just have to hope I was lucky.

I went into the porch, which, I remember, looked cleaner than the façade of the church, but was very bare. I did not mind that. Bareness seemed to me desirable then. I believe I may have sat there for more than a minute. I certainly have the impression of sitting for a time in a small enclosed space. Oddly enough, into this impression also comes the memory of stale cigarette smoke and thick unclean air, so it may be that I compress two memories. This has been suggested to me.

The church door was big and heavy. I would never have believed any door could be so heavy or hard to move. It took me all the strength I had to open it. There are two ways of looking at it: either that door was very very heavy, or I was very weak.

Once inside, I sat down on a bench and closed my eyes, and tried to pray. In fact, I don't remember the prayer, but it must have been in my mind when I entered.

After a little while, I opened my eyes. Something had disturbed me. It was a voice.

'Are you all right? Is there anything I can do?'

I dare say I was a bit surprised at this question. I had always supposed it was the thing to do to sit with your eyes closed in church. At all events, this scene now stands out, like a brilliant cameo, in my mind. 'What denomination are you?' I said.

'What's that?' I registered the surprise in her voice. '*Are* you all right? I mean, you're shaking.'

Now that my eyes were fully open I could see that the interior of the church, so far from being dark and reverent, was full of light from flaring mercury tubes. Desks and tables filled the centre space and invaded the aisles on either side.

'Isn't this a church?' I said.

The woman shook her head. 'Not any longer, no. It was until about three years ago, then it was taken over by the Borough. It's an annexe to the Borough Offices. It's the housing department, in fact. I thought that's why you were here, we do get tenants calling. But if you were looking for a church . . .' she hesitated.

'I didn't know you could defrock a church,' I said stupidly.

'This has been turned over to secular purposes,' she corrected gently. 'You have a special ceremony.'

'I suppose they wouldn't do it to a beautiful church, only an ugly one,' I said.

She looked at me as if I was mad. 'They only secularize redundant churches,' she said. 'It's better than having them fall to bits, isn't it?'

I had come in here looking for darkness and quiet and had come face to face with local government. Across the room someone was humming 'Strangers in the Night'. A telephone rang. I got up to go.

'We've met, haven't we?' said the woman who had been talking to me. 'I'm Yvonne Mitchum. I met you in your office once over a family called Barker, if you remember. We got them a house, but they left London soon after that. They were real wanderers and movers on. I bet they've had people all over the British Isles rehousing them. It was the son that did it. They didn't like to admit that nothing could be done about him. You've only got to look at him to see there's no future for him. Fifteen and still playing with a bowl of beads, I mean that's bad, poor boy.'

'He was a bit retarded.' I remembered the Barkers clearly and Barker was not their real name, I doubt if they themselves remembered what it was. I discovered afterwards that they changed names each time they moved. I knew more about the Barkers than she did, and I had a more particular reason to remember than she could know. The Barkers with their problems belonged to a special time in my life.

'More than a bit,' she said absently. I could see she was giving me a quick professional once-over look. I've done it myself too often to others not to recognize it when it happens to me. Will this one, in any way, cause me trouble? was the question she was seeking an answer to as she looked. I dare say she hardly knew she did it, and she certainly did not know she let it show. I was not willing to dwell on the Barker family or the period of my life with which they were associated, so I started to move away. 'About six years ago it was, I suppose,' she went on. 'Well, he's a man now, whatever that would mean in his case, poor fellow. Wonder what's become of them?' She wasn't worried about me any more, she could see I meant to move on, and so she relented and let me have a titbit of information she might otherwise have held back. 'See that girl over there, sitting at the typewriter? Doesn't she remind you of the Barker daughter? Six years on, of course. I keep thinking it might be her.'

'What's her name?'

'Smith.'

'Could be,' I said, looking at the girl's dark head, bent over her work. 'Why don't you ask her, then?'

'Oh, I couldn't do that.'

The girl at the typewriter looked up; she had a pretty unmemorable face. I didn't think she was Biddy Barker, but it would not have surprised me if she had been. There is a philosophical theory of clusters. Stars cluster in the heavens; lorries cluster on the motorways; events in our lives, too, have a natural affinity. We call it 'good luck' or 'bad luck' according to how the cluster shapes, and talk of things going in threes. Three is a typical cluster. Events of a sad, reminiscent kind were in a cluster about me now.

First, it was meeting Yvonne Mitchum whom I had met six years ago. Then, there was the suggestion that a member of the ill-famed Barker family might be present. And there was the church itself.

'I've been here once before,' I heard myself say. I hadn't intended to say it, but when the words came out I heard them without surprise.

'Oh really?' Yvonne's voice sounded far away.

'When it was a church. It's changed. That's why I didn't remember it at first.'

'Oh, you didn't know?' She sounded doubtful, and rightly so.

'I was only here once ... I'm not ...' I hesitated, 'a worshipper.'

'What did you come to, a wedding or a christening?' she said brightly.

'Neither. It was a funeral.' And suddenly, to my dismay, great rounded tears were flooding down my cheeks. 'It was a funeral.'

It was amazing, really, the way this cluster of events had bunched themselves like a flight of wasps around the point in my life when the way to corruption was opened. Only one tiny slit in the skin is necessary and the wasps are in, opening it and depositing the maggots. For a little while you bear the crack unharmed and walk on. Later, you feel more.

'It all looked so different,' I said again. 'I didn't recognize it.'

Beneath this arch I had stood and smelt incense and the scent of chrysanthemums. I was carrying the flowers tight against my breast, their stylized elegance flattened and crushed, bent into the paper cornet that contained them. I have hated chrysanthemums ever since. The flowers were a mistake, bought on the impulse of the moment, and now, at the funeral service, were an embarrassment. Brides carry flowers in church, not mourners. I had allowed myself to become confused.

After the ceremony the tiny group of people present stood on the steps, while the small coffin was placed in its hearse. I remember standing aside. Two women, one middle-aged, and the priest.

'Three years old, you say?'

'Yes, Father.'

'Poor child, poor child.'

I heard the middle-aged woman murmur something and caught the word 'suffering'.

'Not much of that,' said the other and younger woman. She seemed tearful. 'I did my best, poor little thing, but it had to be. And she was never right, you know, never.'

I had moved forward so that I was standing just behind them. I knew what she meant: that the child had been unlike other children, not so developed. Retarded, if you like. I hated her at the moment.

'I tried my best,' she went on. She dabbed at her eyes.

'You did very well,' said the other, patting her arm. From her manner you might have guessed there was a professional relationship of some sort, not a personal one.

'Yes, Miss Stafford,' said the younger one, dutifully. 'She was adopted, Father, but I loved her as if she was my own.'

'Of course you did,' said Miss Stafford.

'But she couldn't respond, you see, there was just nothing there.'

I thought I had gone unnoticed, but I was wrong. Before they went down the steps to the car, Miss Stafford held back. She turned round to look at me. 'I thought I told you *not* to come,' she said with anger.

'I'm her mother,' I began.

'No,' she said rapidly, stepping down to the waiting car. 'No, not any more.'

That was the moment when my skin was pierced and I was opened up to be eaten. Shortly after the two men approached me with their request, as if they knew I was ready to be devoured.

Afterwards I went back to the office where I worked then (it was a sort of forerunner of the one I am in now) and met the Barker family, so that afternoon their troubles and mine became mixed in my mind.

'It was never very successful as a church, you see,' said Yvonne Mitchum, bringing me back to the present. 'People moved away from the district and the congregation went. And the reason it looks different inside is because it was burnt out. There was a fire about three years ago. Did a lot of damage.' She looked round complacently, as if she had personally supervised the damage and approved of it. 'And so it came to us.'

Even as she spoke I seemed to hear the roar of the flames. Strange how we pluck sounds out of the silent earth and make something real from them. I could hear the roar strongly in my ears as I walked away. My imagination seemed to catch fire with it.

The door to Tim Dean's apartment opened easily. The police said to me did I have a key. I didn't have a key, the door just opened when I turned the handle. This is how I remember it. At some moment I have the impression I first rang the bell and waited, and then, in the next minute, it seems to me that I *knew* the door would open at a touch and that I walked straight in. I remember both actions and it is confusing to me.

107

I went into the sitting-room, which was lit by the afternoon sun shining on the pale leather chair and the cream-coloured Chinese carpet. Timothy had a fine taste in furnishings, although it was perhaps a little old for his years. He was a young man, and this was the sort of furniture that an older man might have chosen. I had been worrying over this thought during my meetings with him, and I still did not know what to make of it. The room was dreadfully disorderly.

I stood there in the middle of the room, then I moved round, picking up displaced objects and trying to tidy up. Such activity was uncharacteristic of me, and I soon stopped.

'Timothy?' I called out.

He appeared at the door. One minute he was seen, the next he was not.

'Science fiction,' I said. 'Yes, *that's* what this is. A science fiction film. You are a man from another planet.'

'I am that,' he agreed. 'Every inch of me.'

'That's how you know to appear so suddenly.'

'I just walked through the door.'

'Did you?' I screwed up my eyes. 'It *looked* like an instant appearance, and that's standard procedure in science fiction.'

'No, this film is more sophisticated, more intellectual.' He was entering into the spirit of it now. 'We are in a space spiral and both of us will soon be thrust into a new world.' His eyes glittered.

'Is that really it? Really? And will these same objects still stand about us?' I looked round the room.

He thought for a moment. 'They may appear to do so for a time, but I believe they will change and become something else. But it will be gradual.'

I waited: there was more to come.

'And we shall change with them.'

I swallowed. 'It sounds horribly lifelike. As if it had happened already.'

'Well, that could be a twist,' he said. 'We *have* been through it all before. That's why it's called a time spiral.'

I sat down on one of his pale chairs. It felt solid enough at that moment, but I suppose it would do. The chair and I and Tim Dean and all our world were made of the same matter, all twirling together up that spiral through space, for ever and ever . . .

'Why didn't we guess it was that sort of film?' I said. 'For a little while I thought it was a love story.'

'Could it not be that too? There has to be a plot.'

'Yes,' I said, sadly, I believe. 'Indeed there has to be a plot. We've told ourselves so many stories and all the time we were just a collection of neutrons and protons rotating in time.'

'Did you see *2001 – Space Odyssey?*' he asked.

'Yes. It was wonderful. It doesn't feel like us, though.' A thought came to me which made me shudder, it seemed so hideously possible. 'Perhaps we are robots. Robots acting out the last Law of Robotics.'

'And what's that?' he asked sceptically.

'To tend towards the human, to develop human feelings. I suppose that's what we've done. I know I have,' I said gloomily. 'Pretty good fun for the viewer, I suppose.'

'This is a tragedy,' he said simply. 'Not a comedy, not a drama, but a tragedy. I didn't want you to know, but it had to come out in the end.'

'Especially if I'm part of it.'

'You don't have to be, dearest Olivia.' He said it kindly, gently. 'We were fellow travellers for a little while. Run away home now, Olivia.'

I watched his face. He was in the grip of some emotion, deeply moved by it. At that moment I thought it might be fear. Had he heard a noise from the other room? I listened but heard nothing. From the next room, nothing.

From then on it was like a film you have seen once before and remember only in parts. In the mirror I saw my face again as I seemed to have seen it several times before.

I looked haggard and tired, which was not surprising. Then I turned towards him again. It was not the hole in the head which somehow I seemed to expect to be there, but his face. Its colour had subtly changed. He was still and cold. I touched his arm and it was rigid.

How can it be, I thought, how can it possibly happen? How can a man be alive, then dead, then stiff, all in such a short space of time?

I leant against the wall and closed my eyes. 'The film is out of sync, the film is out of sync.'

Something had surely gone wrong with the mechanism of time. I was out of life as I knew it, and into Azimov and Vonnegut.

Later I telephoned my sister. There was no answer. I could have telephoned my husband. I had his letter in my pocket. Later still, time still being broken into two for me, I went to the police.

I still thought the story was all about me, that it was my plot, but at this point the scene broke up and the central figure that the audience kept its eyes on shifted to the police.

The story line had changed.

Chapter Nine

From all the faces in a crowd one begins to stand out. All the time, moving about his business, a policeman had been working unnoticed. Now he was to play a vital part in the story. Indeed, his part had always been there, always been important, only unnoticed by some, intent on their own edited version. From his point of view it was partly business, partly a matter of conscience. He had long been aware of Olivia, but Olivia knew little of him. She knew of his existence and had deduced something of his nature, but that was all. He, for his part, had watched Olivia, but had never spoken to her.

He was a policeman called John Coffin, who had been successful and then unsuccessful and was now preparing, with the wary optimism of the native-born cockney, to be successful again. He thought his time had come round again, not because he specially deserved it, or because he had worked towards it, but because that was how the luck went. He could feel it beginning again. He had been a policeman now for twenty-five years and had his ups and downs, and in a way had enjoyed the down as much as the up. There was a freedom and almost an exhilaration in feeling that you were there at the bottom and you could stay there or fight your way back up, the choice was yours. For almost all his years as a policeman he had lived and worked in a suburb of south London. He had married and for a time been very happy and perhaps would be again, but for the moment his wife was working in France and their child was with her. He was an un-conventional policeman, self-educated and tough.

He was still in south London, still working, although no promotion had come his way lately. He knew that somewhere in the large new offices of Scotland Yard was a file on him and he wished he could read it. He supposed there must be a big question-mark in invisible ink on the cover. There were reasons for this assumption.

There had been a time in the days of his first success when all his cases had been odd and had bizarre under-tones. His colleagues used to ask cynically if he attracted the nuts or created them. Cases involving women seemed to fall naturally into his path. The first woman bank robber to escape by means of levitation was one of his. She broke both legs, but made a good recovery.

When he first saw Olivia, at a distance, he saw at once she could become one of his canaries, yet he couldn't help liking her.

'That girl's got trouble written all over her,' he said, unconsciously echoing her sister, who thought the same. 'But what a face. I suppose that's how Deirdre looked, or Cassandra.' He never forgot that first glimpse of her, even when, later on, it was obscured by other pictures. Olivia weeping, Olivia defiant, Olivia defeated, he had it all to come, and so had Olivia.

He had been at the end of a piece of string and Olivia pulled it. On the whole it was to be an experience he would not regret. The string had plucked at him and moved his body as he drank a glass of beer.

Every month he and a group of like-minded men met in a public house called the Falcon. They were all police-men. It was a sort of club, an unacknowledged club of the disaffected. The men who came there were the men who saw things each day in their work and wanted to change them. They met, even in this casual, unobtrusive way, because they gave each other support. Their visits to the Falcon served another purpose: information flowed backwards and forwards between them. They were all of them men who somehow felt troubled at the working of the machine and drew each other's attention to abuse and injustice. They took it for granted that they had a spy among them and were watched. And as time went on even the spy, for there was one, began to wonder if he was spied upon. (In all big organizations spies have other spies to spy upon them.)

Sometimes Coffin wondered if he imagined all this and the group did not really exist as a group, and if all the encounters there were chance and casual and purely social. Perhaps it was just the excellent beer and their common interest in the local football team that brought them to the Falcon; and then someone would say something sharp and Coffin knew there was true tacit purpose in the contacts. The club seemed to have grown up so naturally over a period of five years that it was easy to believe it was of organic growth, but occasionally he wondered if someone was not promoting its growth and if that someone was not him. Probably every group, however inactive, has a more or less conscious begetter.

It was in the Falcon that John Coffin first felt the pull of the string from Olivia. He was drinking, no one was there yet, and he was alone, when he looked up and saw David Short, whom he knew slightly. Like many important occasions it was not heralded in any way. No one sounded trumpets.

'Hello, David.'

'I thought you might be here.'

'Were you looking for me?'

'Not officially.' This was the code word, and the signal for a pause. Coffin looked thoughtful. He had had contacts with David in the past. Between them had passed

113

rough nuggets of information that might cut the fingers of those who handled them.

'Glad to see you,' said David. 'Can we talk?'

'Yes.' Sometimes he felt that David was throwing him biscuits as to an old dog and saying 'trust'.

'A friend of mine, a woman, has a bit of a worry. Her car was stolen. The same day there was a robbery at a post office. Your colleagues *seem* to think her car was used and with her consent. She's sure they want to get her. She wants to know if there really *is* evidence her car was used, or if they are lying.'

'Or even faking it?'

'She doesn't say she suspects them of that. She just thinks they are out to get her,' said David cautiously. 'And what she wants to know is, *is* there any evidence her car was used? You understand, I'm only asking.'

'I could look around,' Coffin said. This was all he said, but it was enough.

'I'll give you her name and the details.' David wrote them down on a small sheet of white paper. Aloud, in speech, he was discreet, but occasionally on paper, he could be direct and unafraid: this was his trade, he was a journalist, a professional loud talker.

'I'll see what I can find out.' Coffin pocketed the paper. 'I know the name.'

'Olivia's pretty well known, one way and another.'

'I suppose so.' He buttoned up his coat and prepared to go. The introduction of Olivia Cooper's name had alerted him. He was on guard. Olivia was known to him as a woman to be watched. She had appeared and then disappeared in various contexts. Was she this or was she that? No one seemed to know. Meanwhile she worked for Shout and had taken part in various more or less harmless demonstrations. Whether she was more or less harmless herself, Coffin wasn't sure.

Before he did anything else, he consulted the file on Olivia that existed in a certain office. It wasn't a thick file. Olivia Cooper, at present living in London. 23 Bermuda Road, N.W.3. (The compiler of the file was more than one address behind Olivia. She had moved twice since he last wrote her up.) Born Belfast, 1944, so she was just a war baby. Married 1st, Edward Devlin, 1965. Marriage ended, 1968. 2nd, James Waverly, 1970. Educated at Queen's University of Belfast, and the London School of Economics, University of London. As a student she had belonged to many political organizations of varying shades of intensity. She had been at one and the same time a member of the Communist Party and the Catholic Church, which seemed to suggest she was a girl of divided loyalties, which was probably the truth. She had also belonged to a nationalist party called Cruithin. None of it seemed serious. But no one could doubt that Olivia herself was a serious person.

There followed a list of the positions Olivia Cooper had held. She had always retained her maiden name professionally, even when technically Mrs Devlin and Mrs Waverly. Come to think of it, and Coffin did think of it, she was still Mrs Waverly. The last page or pages of the file on Olivia Cooper had been removed and a sheet of paper stamped with a message to this effect inserted in their place. Coffin found this exceedingly interesting. He thought he might find Olivia Cooper's name on yet another file somewhere. He had the clear notion that another file of an even more secret nature was being formed on her.

He did, however, check up on the matter of the car which had been stolen, and reported back to David, as David in his turn reported to Olivia, that within the vehicle were indications that the car had indeed been used for the get-away in the robbery and then returned to

115

where Olivia lived. Although why any criminals should have used such a slow and beaten-up old car when they could have stolen a fast Jaguar or Rover was a question to be answered.

This, for the moment, was the end of the episode, but Coffin did not forget Olivia's name. Indeed, he remembered he had heard it before. One day when he was eating in a quiet Italian restaurant whose proprietor, Mr Costello, had once been saved from death by Coffin, Mr Costello had said, 'That's James Waverly, the property developer, and that's his wife.' He looked up and saw her across the crowded room. No one introduced them and he did not then know her name was Olivia, but he was struck by her appearance, which seemed both noble and marvellous and lost, like someone who might die, and die grandly or heroically, for an absolutely pointless cause.

He had put the thought of her aside, but she must have remained there, tenaciously, underneath.

Wednesday was a cold day with rain and to begin with it felt like any other day. Coffin got up, ate his breakfast, put his post in his pocket as he left the house, and took up the day's work. He drank some coffee, then some water, received several telephone calls and let the day's routine sweep over him.

The day went like this:

9.30 – 10.30 a.m.

Read and answer letters. A mixed bag. The letters often contained requests for help and information from other areas. Other letters might contain complaints from residents within his area, or again requests for help and information. (It was surprising, even now, how many people liked to put pen to paper rather than use the telephone.) There might be an anonymous letter and it might be important. Some of his best letters were anonymous. On

116

his desk too, would be probably at least one communication from the Home Office.

10.30 – 11.30 a.m.

The weekly conference with all heads of departments in his crime area. A report on the arson investigation, which was the biggest investigation at the moment. There had been three major warehouse fires within three months. A few minor cases were on hand, too, such as a series of breaking-and-enterings in which the same method of entry was used and only food and money were taken. They also had a nut who was painting walls with white and blue stripes. Or perhaps he was only a man with an eye for colour.

11.30 a.m. – 12 noon.

He had an interview with a probationary detective constable who wasn't going to make the grade.

And so on and so on.

Later in the day, one of his detectives came in grinning and said: 'We've got this bird in here says she's out of Science Fiction.'

Coffin stared. It was a stare on the edge of a glare, that was his first reaction.

'Says she's one of the Sirens of Titan,' said the man seriously.

'That can't be.'

'She means *something* by it.'

'It's a work of fiction.'

'She knows that. She says she never realized until now that she was part of a Purpose. She says she knows her name will be written large on the hills of China.'

Coffin shook his head. 'Has a doctor seen her?'

'No, but she's had a cup of tea and Policewoman Nancy Dream gave her some aspirin.' This was virtually the only drug except caffeine which police regulations allowed the lay hand to administer. 'But when she gave her name we recognized it as one on our special list, and Idden and Hodd want to speak to her. They're on the way.'

The telephone rang to announce their arrival, two thick-set, strong-faced men, very alike in appearance when seen together. When seen apart, you realized they really did have different faces, but the same expression.

'Give us ten minutes,' said Idden, 'and then come in.'

He gave them twenty and then went towards the interview-room. At the reception desk he stopped and said, 'What did you say her name was?'

'One of the names she gave was Medusa,' said the young man, with a straight face.

Coffin was no classical scholar, but he knew Medusa was a girl who turned everyone to stone, and he heard the name with foreboding.

'Of course, it's not her real name,' said the other man hurriedly.

'It could be,' said Coffin. 'It *could* be.'

'Don't unnerve me, boss. *You* don't believe in space-warps and voyagers back from another age.'

'Sometimes I believe in everything,' said Coffin.

It was in this mood he met the woman and recognized her as Olivia Cooper, and at once thought: well, she *is* Cassandra, and Deirdre and Medusa.

Coffin looked across the room and his eyes met Olivia's; they looked sad and distraught as if focused on another world, another place. She seemed like a woman who had been set down in a strange city in a foreign country without a guide-book, and was still looking for the way to go home.

'It's hard to know *what* to make of her,' said Idden. 'I'll get her to go over it and see what you make of it.' He

118

thrust a few written notes over to Coffin. 'Read that, it's the first run-through of what she said, just to put you in the picture.' Then he turned to Olivia, who had been murmuring in a low voice to his sergeant, as if, once started, she could not stop speaking. Now she licked her lips and looked at Idden. 'Say that again. Come on now, you know the bit I mean, don't act stupid. You're not a stupid girl, not by any means. So tell it again. Begin where you went into the kitchen. Or rather just before that.'

'He said I was something much nicer than camouflage. Then I remember feeling hot and tired. Also sick.'

'What made you feel sick?'

'I . . . I don't know. I remember feeling hot and tired. And then I felt sick. Then I took a drink of water. I heard the front door-bell ring. It rings in the kitchen. I called out to him not to answer it . . . I think I called out . . . I think it was then.'

'Did he answer it?'

'I don't know. I don't think so.'

'You were in the next room and the rooms actually connect and you don't know if he answered the doorbell?'

'I don't know.'

'Did the bell ring again?'

'I believe it did. I'm confused. It rang later . . . later.'

'Go on, you drank some water, then what?'

'I drank some more water. When I went back to the room, I found him dead.'

'Are you sure he was dead?'

'He was stiff and dead.'

When Olivia had been taken away, one policeman turned to the other.

'Well, what do you make of that?'

The other man was deliberate. 'She's not a liar. I'm sure she believes she's telling the truth?'

'How could she be?'

'Yes, that's right.' He picked up a cigarette. 'How could she be? The laws of physics would have to be contradicted.'

'Physics?'

'The thermodynamics of the body solids, the changed state of the body liquids as they cool. I suppose it's a form of physics? A physical law, anyway.' He lit the cigarette. 'How could a man be alive one minute and rigid dead the next?'

'I wouldn't take her seriously for a moment,' said Idden, 'if it wasn't for the Creamery Road Post Office do. But having got my hands on her, I don't want to let her out of them.'

'I suppose the whole thing could be fantasy,' said Coffin. 'Didn't strike me that way, though . . . Anyone had a look at Davenport Road yet?'

'I asked for a car to go and check, and with your permission I will get the report here.'

Coffin did not even bother to answer. These Special Branch men overrode all boundaries and were not under his authority. It was mere politeness which made Idden speak now, and even that was thinly laid on. There was no friendliness between the men. In Coffin's view it was impossible to like either of them, they had a special psychology which either was drilled into them or was why they were recruited. He felt poles apart from Idden. Indeed, he wondered idly, not really caring as much as he should, if Idden was checking on *him* too. It seemed possible.

They were sitting there, without having spoken much more, when the call came through from the driver of the police car which had gone to Davenport Road. Coffin took the call. The man had a cheerful voice on the telephone and sounded pleased, as though he had done well.

'It's all right,' he said loudly, so that the other two men could hear easily. 'Nothing there. Whole place is as clean

120

as a whistle. I got in, had a quick look round. It's a bit untidy but no body. Certainly no body in the bed. In fact the bed's made up and tucked in.' He made it sound cosy. 'She's having you on.'

Coffin and Idden stared at each other. 'I half expected this,' said Idden slowly.

'I didn't,' said Coffin.

'Let's ask her to come back in and see what she says.'

'Perhaps she'll give a merry laugh and say the clouds have rolled away,' said Hodd.

Coffin disagreed. He would have disagreed anyway with Hodd, but he could do so with conviction now. 'She's not a joker.'

Idden nodded. 'No. I'm with you there. She's almost without humour.'

'Do you think it's just a complete fantasy that she made up?'

'Could be. She's in a very strung-up, unnatural state. Or she could have been instructed to tell us that story.'

'Instructed?' Coffin queried.

'Told to do it. I'm almost sure she's directed by someone. On behalf of some illegal organization.'

'Which one?' said Coffin. Idden did not answer. So all right, thought Coffin, no answer, and he determined to find out which organization his colleague meant. 'She gave me the impression she *believed* what she was saying.'

'Let's tell her the good news and see what she does.'

They waited.

But when they had Olivia in and told her that in the flat at Davenport Road there was no body, she stared at them wide-eyed for a moment.

'He's not there? So it *was* another world, another time, and I was right all the time.' And then she fainted.

'She tells you everything and nothing, that girl,' said Idden, exasperated.

121

The police matron who helped revive her reported to Coffin and Idden that she suspected Olivia to be under the influence of some drug as well as emotionally strained.

'There are some pricks on her wrist,' she reported dispassionately.

The strange thing was that after she had fainted Olivia seemed much better, altogether more rational and composed, as if the shock had been good for her. This was at once apparent to Coffin, although the other men, not so sensitive to Olivia, did not seem to notice it.

If there had been a fantasy playing itself out in her mind, she was over it now. He watched her closely and was convinced of it. He wondered if it had been drug-induced. She didn't look like an addict. She didn't look mad, either, but you could never tell.

'Do you mind, John?' Idden was speaking to him, and the use of the Christian name was a cynical friendliness that was not endearing. 'I'd like just a few words with Miss Cooper ...' On his own he meant, and you, dear John, outside the door.

'Of course.' Coffin left the room, closed the door quietly and stood there for a moment, listening. Not for the first time, he wished he had the room bugged. There was something disturbing about Idden and his concentration on Olivia. He himself was being excluded, and he knew it.

He caught a few words, and perhaps was even meant to hear them. Enough to tell him that Idden was putting questions to her about her motor-car and her knowledge of the men who had raided the post office in Creamery Road, who had made away with a few hundred pounds and had shot a man who had since died. What Olivia was answering, if indeed she was answering, was inaudible.

The interview seemed to come to an end rapidly, and

Olivia emerged. She looked tired, but sane. Her questioner, Idden, looked cross; no doubt about it, he was put out. Whatever it was he wanted, he hadn't got it.

Olivia appeared sad as well as sane. Somehow the combination of the two made her look authentic and Idden a charlatan, which was not the way it ought to be at all. People like Olivia had no business to look like saints, and policemen had no business to look dishonest.

She went out through the door as if she was walking into oblivion.

Five minutes later, when she was walking along the busy main road leading west, a car drew up. For a moment, she looked frightened.

'Get in,' said Coffin, briskly. 'I'll take you wherever you want to go.'

'That's nowhere,' said Olivia.

'We shall get there quickly,' said Coffin imperturbably. 'The traffic usually makes good speed in that direction.'

'Oh, funny man.'

'Good, you are alive, then. I thought a talk between us two might be a good idea. Odd, you turning up there like that.' He drove on. 'Even wondered if you might be some sort of a trap for *me*.'

She looked up.

'We have something in common, you know, you and I. Some friends like David Short and Tony Tomlinson, for instance.'

'Oh,' said Olivia, making it a long sound.

'Yes, oh. So I know a bit about you.'

'I'm not an *agent provocateur*,' said Olivia.

'No, I know that now.' He slowed the car. 'All the same, you owe me something. You owe me an explanation. What *were* you doing this afternoon? Tell me. Talk.'

Outside the car the crowded pavements slid past. It was

still early enough for the shops to be open and busy. Olivia stared out at them. She kept her face turned away. She began in the middle.

'When I was walking along I thought I must disburden myself. I must *tell*. I must tell about this man lying dead ... So, I found a Police Station and I started to tell ... I was still muddled, but I swear I tried to tell as things are. As I believed ... That's all. Now are you satisfied?'

'Hardly that, but very very interested. It's a good and interesting story you tell.'

'When I told it to that detective Idden he listened in a funny sort of way ... He listened to me as though he had heard it all before.' She looked at Coffin. 'As if it was a story he had read in a book. *Could* he have?'

'Don't you *know*?'

There was a moment's pause: she shook her head.

'You're a funny funny girl,' said Coffin.

They drove on in silence and then he spoke again. 'Let's suspend judgement for a little while. Let's go and visit this flat in Davenport Road and see for ourselves. Have you got a key?'

'No, no key. I used to ring or else the door used to open when I turned the handle.'

'I see.' It sounded unlikely.

He continued to drive across London. Olivia sat by his side, quietly observing the streets, almost as if she was enjoying it. It occurred to Coffin that she was exhausted and glad of the rest. He looked at her.

Olivia took a deep breath. 'Do you think I'm mad? It would be mad to have that sort of nightmare.'

'Do you take drugs?' he said bluntly.

'Well, I've tried a bit of this and that. Who hasn't?' He did not react to this: he was not required to. She was troubled, though, as if he had hit on a question to which there was more of an answer than she wanted to give. He

124

saw her draw her cuffs down over her wrists and then rest her hands primly in her lap. A little frown appeared.

'Are you on anything now?'

She shook her head. 'No. Honestly . . . I heard what the policewoman said and I know what you think, but it's not so.'

He left it at that. Fantasies such as she had brewed up could come from a bad trip. Perhaps she *had* even killed a man and left him somewhere.

He drove on. On the way, they passed a small park. A boy with a dog was walking along the pavement by the park, looking at all the motor-cars lining the kerb. The dog was straining at the leash, but the boy refused to hurry. Davenport Road looked very normal when they got there, not as if it had witnessed any violence. He watched her to see how she took the sight of the road. She took it well, interested, alert and a little tense, thus easily passing a little test he had put up for her.

He parked the car at the kerb and stood looking up at the smart block of flats which had been created from a 1930s mansion. 'Nice place,' he said.

'Yes, it is.'

He waited, and without hesitation Olivia led the way into the entrance hall. She seemed quite familiar with the entrance. 'She *has* been here before.' She advanced to the door of a ground-floor flat, and he watched her put out a hand to the door knob. The knob seemed to turn slightly, but the door did not open.

'I can't get in,' she said.

He waited for a minute, wondering if she would produce any solution. Then: 'We could ring the bell,' he suggested.

He watched her push the door-bell gently, almost shyly. No one answered. He wondered what she would have done if someone had come.

125

'We know it's empty or was when the police patrol-car called,' he reminded her.

'How did the policeman get in?'

'There are ways. I expect he had a look round and then quietly took one.' He was looking round himself as he spoke. At the back of the entrance hall was a glass door giving light and also opening on to a small paved court with garages behind. He went through, Olivia following. He looked around the courtyard. The flats above had windows that overlooked it, but otherwise blank walls faced it.

'Go back in,' he said to Olivia, 'and wait.'

'What for?' She sounded nervous.

'For me.' He gave her a push. She went back in and shut the glass door behind her. In a little while Coffin re-appeared at the front door of the flat. He had climbed in through a back window and walked through, following in the footsteps, he suspected, of the other policeman.

'Come in,' he said, holding the door open, 'and be quiet.'

Slowly Olivia walked inside, and he closed the door behind her. She was white and holding her coat closely about her, as if she was cold. It was warm inside the place, and the air smelt stale. There was another smell on the air which he had not yet identified, but it was not the smell of death. After a little while he realized it was the smell of after-shave lotion, and that did surprise him. He watched Olivia, she did not seem to notice, not everyone had a keen sense of smell. It suggested a living man to him and not a dead one.

Olivia walked into the middle of the sitting-room, and stood there in silence. The silence grew.

'Notice anything?' said Coffin.

The room was tidy, the furniture polished, the cushions lying neatly against the pale leather. Olivia moved slowly round the room, her expression troubled. At one point she went over to a cupboard and looked inside. There was nothing there except some clean glasses and a bottle of Vichy water. In one corner of the room was a desk, with a sloping lid. She tried to open it, but it was locked.

'You've had a look round?' she said to Coffin.

'Before I let you in.'

'Stay here,' she said, commanded almost. Coffin felt it would not do to disobey. Within the next few minutes she conducted a swift tour of the flat, then she returned to where Coffin still stood. Her coat, no longer clasped, was hanging open.

'Nice place,' he said. 'Notice anything?'

She hesitated. 'It looks different.'

'You didn't want to say that, did you?'

'No.'

'So what's different?'

'Things here and there. It's like and yet not like.' She looked at him with sad big eyes.

'I'll tell you one thing that's different,' Coffin said. He put his arm round Olivia and drew her towards the door of one of the other rooms and made her face it. 'No bed.'

She turned her head stiffly away. 'There's a divan.'

'It's not a bed, it's a thin narrow divan. Look at it and say if you recognize it.'

Her answer stumbled. 'I . . . don't know.'

'Do you still say you were in this place and met a man here and made love to him and eventually found him dead?'

Without wanting to cry and perhaps without knowing it was happening she found tears forming in her eyes. 'I don't know . . . I seem to know the place . . . In some ways I do, and in other ways it seems strange . . . The whole thing begins to seem unreal.'

'As if you imagined it?' he pressed.

127

'No . . . not imagined. As if I saw it happening outside myself . . . like a film I was watching.'

Coffin took her wrist and turned it so that the prick marks on the soft skin on the inside were clearly visible. 'Just what are those?' he said.

Olivia drew back her arm. 'I'm not sure. I didn't do it. Perhaps an insect bit me.'

'No insect bites like that. You're in big trouble, Olivia, aren't you?'

'Yes,' she said. 'I feel as if when I really wake up I'll remember it all and it will be terrible.'

'I wouldn't be surprised,' said Coffin. 'You look to me like a girl who's had a fair beating about.'

A look of surprised horror flashed across Olivia's face, and her hand flew to her throat.

'A moment of awaking memory?' he asked sardonically.

'Yes, just then I thought: but I *did* get beaten.' The shadow of a bruise seemed to deepen and thicken on her cheek. She threw out her hands in a gesture of despair. 'I don't know whether to hope it was all a dream, or hope it was not. Either way I'm done for.' She went round the room slowly touching the furniture piece by piece. 'I do know this, I have seen it all before. I'm not so crazy.'

'We'd better be off.' Coffin was more alive than she seemed to be to the possibility of someone walking in and finding them there. For some time now he had been on the alert, listening.

'If you say so.' Olivia took a last look round and then, with a little shake of her head, walked towards the door, hands thrust into her pockets.

Then she stopped short. 'Oh, silly Olivia, stupid forgetful Olivia.' She drew her left hand slowly from her pocket with a small white card in it and held it towards him. 'Look.'

He took it and read: Timothy Dean. Archibald Press. The address, Davenport Road, was underneath, and a message was written in pencil on the back. He read the message silently, then handed it back.

'No comment,' he said.

'You don't *believe*?'

He shrugged. 'Well, it's not so easy to put into words as that.'

'I'm walking a tightrope, and on either side there's a rotten great abyss.'

'Keep walking,' said Coffin. 'And if you think that's flip I'm telling you, it's not, it's good advice. In fact, we'll take a step or two now.' He looked at his watch. 'Nearly five-thirty. Offices will be closing but might be still open. Let's telephone the Archibald Press and see what they have to say about Mr Timothy Dean.'

'He's away on business,' said Olivia quickly, then clapped a hand over her mouth.

'*Is* he?' Coffin gave her a quick look, as he picked up the telephone and dialled. 'Stand close and listen.'

A girl's voice said: 'Archibald Press.'

'May I speak to Mr Timothy Dean? You do have a Mr Timothy Dean?'

'Oh yes. He's back.'

He turned the receiver so that Olivia could hear. 'I'm getting through. They say he's there.'

Presently they heard a man's voice, mellifluous, beautiful, absolutely unmistakable. Once heard it would not be forgotten.

'Timothy Dean here.'

Coffin looked at Olivia. Slowly she shook her head. He put the receiver down.

Without another word passing between them they went out of the apartment into the outer hall. They were on the point of leaving when they heard footsteps coming down the stairs from the floor above. Coffin put his arm under Olivia's elbow to hurry her, but unaccountably she dragged back. She turned her head towards the stairs, she wished to see who came down them.

A tall, slender elderly woman appeared, nodded politely at them and passed them to go out of the door. She was wearing a violet cloth coat trimmed with dark fur and a paler violet hat. A breath of sweet scent passed with her. She looked elegant, worldly and detached. At the door she paused to take some letters from a box labelled 'Delacour'. A name which seemed to suit her.

'Know her?'

Olivia shook her head. Her eyes filled with tears.

'I'd better take you home.' He thought about this for a moment. 'Do you have a friend you could go to?'

'There's Lally. Louise Ashley, my best friend. I could go there.'

Lally received Olivia with affection, but uneasily. Coffin thought that, although obviously concerned and wishing to help, she did not want Olivia with her. This was understandable when you saw the state of her home. Miss Ashley lived in high-class squalor. It was clean, he admitted, but Lally wasted her possessions and also herself. She had many lovely things there, but they were none of them in order. Lally was a *truly* extravagant person in that she abused her treasures. Beautiful and neglected objects were scattered round her room as if abandoned by a barbarian caravan that had passed through, spilling its valuables unheeded as it went. There was a canary singing wildly in a tiny gilded cage covered with enamelled plaques and china flowers. It was a toy that Jeanne Antoinette de Pompadour might have owned. The canary was singing, but had lost its delicate porcelain head: someone had knocked it off. You could see the head at

130

the bottom of the cage, laid away for safety in an old match-box. She had what looked like a Mayan deity with a kicked-in nose, acting as a door-stop. Clothes, gay and vivid, rich and silky, hung everywhere. In the centre of it all stood a golden bed shaped like a swan. Leda *would* be her image, thought Coffin, who knew women like Lally and knew that godhead turned her on. A natural-born betrayer if I ever saw one, he thought, and he doubted if Olivia had any idea of it. But she would find out.

Olivia did not introduce them and seemed, indeed, to have forgotten she had Coffin with her. She embraced Lally and sat down on a chair and stared in front of her. Lally fluttered around, trying to make contact.

'I believe she's coming round and will probably be more herself soon. I'd get her to bed if you can.'

'I'll heat a hot-water bottle,' said Lally. 'What's the matter with her?'

Coffin thought for a moment. 'She's not in her right mind,' he said carefully. 'For reasons I'm not quite clear about.' Either that or she's a tremendous liar, he added to himself.

He left them together, leaving behind him no name and no address. If Olivia wanted him she knew where to find him.

When he got home, he opened a letter from his wife, telling him that she would never be returning home, that she had other plans for the future and that a divorce must be arranged. To his own surprise he was not in the least unhappy.

Next day Olivia left Lally's, returned to her own flat, went to work and took up her life as usual. She saw visitors, and on the next day, after her return to work, she lunched with her husband and her secretary Sarah.

Coffin wondered what she was thinking about.

*

A week passed.

There was no doubt about it, Olivia was a girl with a purpose now. Coffin kept an unobtrusive watch on her and was sure of it. But what that purpose was he could not make out. She looked much the same. Her clothes were always ill chosen, so there was nothing different there. She had dug an old fur coat out of somewhere and wore it all the time. The weather had turned cold so her appearance did not stand out. But inside the fur she looked pinched and thin. And very resolute.

One day she went to her local library and after half an hour came out bearing an armful of books. Judging by the expression on her face she was not going home for an evening's escapist reading. The detective who had observed her while out on another job told Coffin that they were books of different types, and he knew the names of several, having been gifted with particularly long sight. She had chosen books by Elizabeth Daly, Gore Vidal, Kurt Vonnegut and Dashiell Hammett.

The next day she went to the National Film Archive and was gone for hours. She was only noticed this time because a watch was being kept on all public buildings owing to a terrorist bomb alert. The next day Coffin went in and enquired what films she had asked about. Her task was the easier because she knew a man who worked there. Olivia, he reflected, would always know someone working where she wanted help or information. In spite of her friendless air she had ways of getting help. Look at the way she had found him. It didn't anger him, it made her seem young and touching. She had told her friend at the Film Archive that she was doing a study of violence in films and he had run through the reels of certain selected films. She had looked at *The Maltese Falcon*, the bit where the young killer is first seen clearly, and then the final reel where the two lovers, mutual betrayers, confront

132

each other. She had stayed with this some time. Then she had a look at *Strangers on a Train*, and it seemed to interest her. Was it Hitchcock or Raymond Chandler or Patricia Highsmith that she was studying? Then she tried to find a film called *Kiss Me Deadly*, but they didn't have that. She fumbled around through the catalogue for a bit, and then she sat and talked to her friend there about the plots and stars of old films. She had examined one or two stills, turned over old picture magazines and walked round an exhibition they were running on 'Design in the Movies, from 1920 to 1945: the Twenty-Five Golden Years'. She hadn't talked much but lingered around the display-case showing off early science-fiction films, and she had hung over some material from musicals of the thirties, famous ones like *Top Hat*, but this was probably just for fun.

After a while Coffin became convinced that she was looking for the face of a dead man.

He was pursuing two parallel paths in his interest in Olivia. On the one hand there was his own study of her; on the other he took every chance of talking to Inspector Idden. He felt a wry pleasure in that. Idden made it so easy, so sickeningly easy, that he knew Idden was out for information on *him* and was wondering what knot bound Coffin and Olivia together. No knot, he wanted to say, except that at the moment we are both at odds with the world in which we find ourselves. Perhaps the trouble was that they were both of them designed to be out-at-elbows people and could never fit in with any state of things that required of them sleek living and prosperity.

He saw Idden twice in the next few days while Olivia was abroad in London, apparently sane and well.

'We don't know as much about her as I'd like,' said Idden. 'Nor about you,' said his frown, expressive in his inexpressive face. 'We know that she has belonged to any number of fringe societies. She always seems mixed up with the trouble-makers, but never actually one of them.'

Coffin nodded, this was something of his view too. Only time would show how much Olivia herself agreed with it. It seemed likely that she thought of herself as a dangerous person. And she might be right.

'And yet you always know a bit more than you admit to,' suggested Coffin, and his colleague's modest smile admitted that this could be the case. Coffin was careful to sound as impersonal as possible. 'Funny business,' he said. 'Says she doesn't use drugs. I think she's had a shock of some kind. What did you think?'

'We were watching her, had been doing so in a preliminary kind of way for some time. More intensively since her car was used in the robbery.'

'If you were watching her then you ought to know something about whether her story is true or not.'

Idden spread out his hands. 'You'd think so, wouldn't you? But not enough. Our watcher tells us she certainly did call at the house in Davenport Road, but he doesn't know what she was doing there. On the one occasion when he walked up the steps and had a look she was still standing in the hall. Perhaps she never did more than that.'

'A real fun time for her,' said Coffin sourly. He hated the picture of Olivia standing desolate in that hallway.

'Depends on her motivation,' said Idden, who occasionally picked up a word he liked and spun it round on his tongue, enjoying it. In his mouth motivation sounded most sinister. 'She may have been instructed to do all she did. We've been told she responds very well to direction.' This, too, appeared to be a word he savoured, and he lingered on it for a moment.

'And who is directing her?'

'When she was a student she joined a group called Cruithin.'

'What's that?'

'It's the ancient Irish name for the original inhabitants of Ireland, probably of the whole British Isles. Picts, they were called elsewhere. The aims and ambitions of this society, which may at one time have been quite large, were to destroy the English connection with Ireland. Devlin, her first husband, belonged to Cruithin. Cruithin was later dissolved or possibly went underground and linked up with a very much more violent Association.'

He didn't want to give emphasis to the last word, but he had been so long in the business that he gave it a capital letter without noticing. He was so much involved with people who had a cause that a little of it had rubbed off on him. 'She's divorced from that first husband, Devlin; he's a violent man, but I think he still has a hook in her.'

'Do they meet, then?'

Idden shrugged. 'They communicate. They may meet. She's still an active member, I'm convinced. That's why we are watching her. She came to our attention earlier and we've kept an eye on her ever since. I've always had the feeling with her that she'd lead us to something.'

'And so she has, but where?'

'They gave her a job, I think.'

'What job?'

Idden shook his head. 'I don't know. Could be just the use of her car. It's our theory that the robbery was staged to get funds for their organization. But the use of her car looks more like an attempt to implicate her. It would give them a hold over her – blackmail, if you like. I know she's been frightened, know she tells lies, has secrets. I even know what people have secrets from her.' He threw out his hands. 'All this I know about her, but the central mystery escapes me.'

'Yes, you do know a lot.'

'I've read her diary. Her friend, Miss Ashley, with whom she had left it for safe keeping, was induced to part with it. I'll let you see a copy. She has a sort of code that she uses, but a baby could decipher it.'

Coffin recoiled. 'It seems an invasion of privacy.'

'My dear chap, one or other of us has been reading it all the last few days. Can't keep away. She's still writing in her diary, too. She keeps it up to date. When she goes out one of my operatives goes in and photographs what's new. Every time I switch off from something else I find myself thinking about what she's written. An invasion of privacy? Let me tell you it works both ways. *She* invades *you.*'

So Coffin read her diary, not then, but later in the day, beginning in the middle of a sentence going on to *Before I knew what they were about they had me off the 9.20 train from Harrow to Euston and on to the train named Corruption.*

At the end of it he did not know what to make of Olivia. Every word she wrote had the ring of truth but the truth she wrote of was one that could hardly bear the scrutiny of the light of day.

It was unreasonable. Coffin was, in many ways, a simple man and he believed that what was unreasonable could not be. But Idden was correct: Coffin had put a foot inside Olivia's world and could not now walk out unless she gave him leave.

The next day two men were taken from a lodging-house in St Luke's Road (behind St Luke's Church, now used as municipal offices) and driven to a police station in the neighbourhood. After an overnight stay they were charged with being concerned in the robbery with murder which had taken place at the Creamery Road Post Office.

136

It was said that a woman was also wanted in connection with this crime, but had not yet been arrested.

It was nothing to do with Coffin, but he was not the only one watching the news and David Short telephoned him to find out if the woman wanted was Olivia and to warn him that, if it was, he would be taking up her case. 'Does she say she is innocent?' asked Coffin, who really wanted to know.

'She doesn't say anything,' was the answer. 'She's stopped talking. Remember, I'm counting on you.'

David Short also telephoned Idden, who then made a call to Coffin suggesting he call off Short and his colleague Tony Tomlinson. It was a significant call, revealing for the first time that Coffin's little group of dissidents were marked men. It was only what he had already guessed. However, he decided to visit the Falcon that evening and pass the warning round. It might help some of them. His own career, such as it was, he thought, was over.

It was almost entirely his own work, but Olivia had made a contribution. He had to find out if she was worth it.

Olivia saw him sitting in his car before he saw her. She emerged from her office, saw the car at the kerb and came over, moving quickly.

'You've been following me,' she said.

'No.'

'Yes, you have. Well, someone has. What is it you call it – a tail?' Her voice sounded light and ironic, like a character in a well produced comedy; he wondered what sort of effect the books and films she had been studying had had on her. 'And you telephoned David Short.'

'No, he telephoned me.'

'I think he wants me for a martyr.' And she added, 'I

137

may oblige him yet. I'm working on it.' She got into the car.

'Will you let me drive you home?'

'Don't you have a home yourself?'

'No.' And the minute he had said it, he knew it was true and he did not care. He and Olivia could be homeless and timeless together. They could step off on a cloud and disappear into space. He began to move the car slowly and carefully away, as if, with proper concentration, their air-lift might come any minute now.

'First, there are some things you must understand. To begin with, you must understand that I am a serious person. And when I was asked to accept that what had been for me a period of tragedy was really a period of comedy, farce even, it came hard. Even now I find it hard to accept.' She swallowed, almost as if nausea was not far away. 'Well, so what happened to me was a fantasy, something I dreamed up. Why?' She stared at her wrists.

'Drugs? A bad trip?'

'I don't remember taking anything. I suppose someone could have given it to me. A rotten trick.'

Coffin thought of Lally, and wondered.

'You don't know,' went on Olivia. 'I've been going through a bad time. I've been apart from my husband for some time now. You know that, no doubt. But I discovered recently,' she paused, 'that he wants to marry again. A girl I know. Nice girl.'

Coffin waited.

'Of course, it's not important. *Public* life is important, not what one does privately.'

'That's your philosophy?'

She looked at him. 'It's what I've always believed; it's what I've acted on. My relationship with the group – I won't use the word society – is what matters, not my relationship with my husband.'

'If you lived like that, I don't wonder that your fantasies put hats on and started to walk around in your life.'

'You think that's what happened?'

He was silent. He knew that the independent watch on her kept by Idden's men suggested that some element in her story had actually happened. She *had* gone to the flat in Davenport Road; she was under pressure from men who might have attacked her. 'I don't know,' he said. 'I think you got a dose of a drug from somewhere and it's had a strange effect on you.'

'One way and another, I had a sort of breakdown,' she said. 'I lost faith in myself and my own observation. That *is* the way of madness.' She laughed. 'You've got to believe what everyone else believes, haven't you, or you *are* mad.'

'You're not mad,' said Coffin.

'Let's say I was put in a mad situation, then. I like that "was put", don't you? It suggests it was more than my doing. And perhaps it was not. Perhaps I really did wander out of my little bit of time and space and into something else. Perhaps all the things I saw haven't happened yet but are going to happen.' She turned and looked up at Coffin.

He shook his head slowly from side to side. 'No.'

An uneasy expression appeared on Olivia's face, as if she was looking back to a time when she had put a question like that once before and got a very different answer.

'I have this picture of a dark place with one light hanging from the ceiling . . . It reminds me of, in fact, it *looks* like the landing of the staircase outside my flat, but it can't be. And I'm leaning up against the wall and a man is facing me and another one is holding my arm and then in my arm he puts a hypodermic syringe and someone is saying "liar, liar". It must be from a film, I suppose. Or else I imagined it. But it seems so real.' Her voice fell

139

away. 'And after that, nothing was real, it was all out of sync, as if the projector and the sound track had lost touch with each other and anyway were telling a different story. Silly, isn't it?'

'That was no film.'

She stared.

'It was real. Or you thought it was real. You wrote it all out in your diary. As if it happened to you.'

'But my husband found me on the stairs.'

'You were just going back to get your handbag, which had fallen there. You say so yourself in the diary.'

'My diary,' she flushed. 'You've read it? But it's in code.'

'It was easy to read.'

Olivia turned and gave him a long hard look. '*How* do you know?'

'Lally. Your dear friend Lally. She let Idden take a copy. You should never have left your writings with her.'

'Well, then,' said Olivia, 'you know all my sad story.' She managed, even then, to keep her voice level. 'But I'll probably kill Lally.'

'No.' He put a hand on her cold, clenched fist. 'No more talk of killing.'

'What did he give her?'

'Nothing much, I suppose. Lally is an easy betrayer. She's probably done it to you before.'

'I wrote things there that meant a lot to me,' said Olivia. 'But perhaps I always wanted it to be read. Perhaps it was one of those cries for help we all give at some time. Not you, of course, *you* don't call for help. I suppose you know it's of no use. In the end you are on your own. That's what you learn. If you need to learn it. Probably the wise ones do not. Well, I'd like you to know that I've tried to help myself.'

'And how have you been doing that?'

140

'I've been looking for a face, a plot that I could have used to build up my little story. I'm a great romancer, you know, and I thought I'd made myself this drama out of someone else's old business. And I think I did, too.'

'You found something?'

'Yes. Not what I expected, though.'

Coffin said nothing; he was watching. He could see by her face she was coming to a decision. 'Drive me home, and I'll show you,' she said.

On arrival in that seedy retiring place she called her home (and no home was ever less homelike) Olivia threw her coat on a chair which already housed a dressing-gown and a tweed skirt and invited Coffin to sit on a battered chaise-longue of ancient elegance. She poured some sherry into a delicate piece of Victorian glass and offered it to him with the grace of Hebe handing out nectar.

'All this time I've been reading books and looking at old films and studying magazines, my source material you might call it, because I thought maybe his face, or even just the turn of his head, or else something he *said* would stare at me from a film shot or a book and I would know where I got it all from. Because I have the very strong feeling I did not invent it all.' She stared at him earnestly. 'Underline that, will you, *I did not invent it all.*' She poured herself some sherry in a thick glass beer-mug. 'Perhaps I plucked a man from here, a story-line from there, a bit of dialogue from memory, and built it all up like a dream.'

'Could be,' said Coffin, watching her lovely face.

'But you think not? It's how the mind, the eclectic mind works.' She was rummaging in a pile of magazines.

'Don't take too much of that sherry,' he said.

She had finished her search and held in her hand what

141

she wanted to find, and was turning over the leaves, faster and faster.

'Look here.' She opened the pages at a double colour-spread. 'Here it is.'

The magazine was a thick glossy production called *Home-Maker*, the last sort of periodical Olivia seemed likely to read. 'I've had this over a year,' she said feverishly. 'It dates from the days when I was living with my second husband, he has a lovely house.' Her tone was detached: it was *his* house, and not hers. 'The time-lag explains why I had forgotten. Or not quite forgotten, it appears.'

He looked. There, before him, in colour, most carefully photographed, and captioned 'An Apartment to view: this week's chosen decor', were spread the sitting-room and bedroom of the flat in Davenport Road.

He raised his head. 'Do you think you built the whole thing up from these pictures?'

'It has to start somewhere. But what I will never know now is where *he* came from and that makes me very very sad, because whether you believe it or not, I loved him.

'I wonder where he came from and where he has gone?' she went on, her face rapt. 'Back into the past, or lying waiting for me in the future?'

Coffin put his arm round her. He thought he had never seen a stranger expression on a living face. 'He wasn't there, was he? You know that now. He was never there at all.'

'Yes,' she said doubtfully.

'You imagined it.'

'I imagined it? I suppose so.'

'Hang on to that,' said Coffin.

The next day the body of a young man was found in the bedroom of the flat in Hammersmith where he had lived for three months. He was found by his landlord. He had been dead for some time. The landlord said he had been alerted by the uncollected bottles of milk which had accumulated. The milkman said he had been delivering milk for the last eight days, having responded to a pre-arranged signal that he would start delivering milk again when an empty milk bottle was placed outside.

Chapter Ten

My name is Timothy Dean, and I came back home one day, after a few weeks' absence on business, and there is this man in bed in my flat and he's dead. Very dead. Shot. Through the head.

My God, I think, it's like the beginning of a thriller, say an American film thriller of the late 1930s, and utterly incredible. I mean, we're all more sophisticated now, aren't we, and you don't find bodies in your bed, they turn up in more likely spots like the gutter, in a crashed motor-car. Only I did find this body.

It began like that for me. All these thoughts dashed through my head sooner than I could put tabs on them. I was incredulous and angry, but the thing had happened. 'Why *me*? Why *here*?' I found myself saying.

In a little while I plucked up courage to have another look, a longer one, at the body, and I saw it was my young cousin Teddy.

It was a shock. He'd been in enough trouble, God knows, but I'd never expected it to come to this. And I was fond of the young beggar. I even admired him. I never thought it would come to this. I could not believe he had committed suicide. And in such a manner, too; he was not, I knew, a physically brave man.

I got myself out of the bedroom and shut the door, and leaned against it. It was a disaster, and I knew I could not let him stay where he was.

It was absolutely imperative that there should not be a

body in my bedroom in the next week. The body of a stranger would be bad enough, but the body of a relative would sink me.

I would have to move him. I was well aware that this was a criminal act and probably a sin. But the duty of self-preservation is laid on us as well, is it not, by the church and by natural law. I would utter some heartfelt prayers and offer myself a special dispensation. I took courage and went back into the room.

A distressing thought was that he was dead in my bed. I had had the bed specially built for me and I knew it was a mistake the minute it was delivered. Flynn put his finger on it at once. 'It's not *like* you,' he said. 'It's not *you* at all.' But I already knew. It was too heterosexual, that bed. It had lust written all over it. What I had been aiming at was a delicate, whimsical, withdrawn effect, a chaste couch.

Now, with my poor cousin in it, the bed looked like something out of an engraving by Hogarth. I sat down and studied them. 'Well, nothing can bring him back,' I thought. 'But something has got to take him away.'

I had to do it decently. It was absolutely beholden on me to make the move with dignity. Fortunately, in spite of being tall and slim, I am a strong man with well developed muscles. I keep myself in trim with a weekly set of dynamic exercises. When Flynn saw me at work upon them, he said: 'But you're doing the exercises laid down for *women*.'

'It's of no significance,' I at once replied to Flynn. It never does to let him step too far out of line. I owe it to myself as the older person to retain a dominant position if I can. The balance between us is very even as it is. And, as a matter of fact, the feminine exercises suit me best. There's no doubt that since doing Crocus, Cactus and Catkin regularly my waist and tummy muscles are really

145

taut. More to the point in my present predicament, my trapezius muscles round my neck and shoulders ripple. Also, breathing freely in the lion (with mouth open) position has greatly helped my wind. I anticipated no physical problems in carrying off my poor cousin, although mental and moral questions must remain.

For a moment I considered using Flynn's taxi, but I dismissed the idea. He's a perfectly charming person, but discreet he is not. Nor could I be sure what line he would take. Like all people of his age he sometimes adopts a very hard moral stance. Nor did I think he was above punishing me a bit. Flynn and my cousin were much of the same age; Flynn would identify with Teddy and say, 'Why should this poor B be moved from where he died just because his body will be an embarrassment to you?'

More than an embarrassment: a disaster, the end of the upward thrust of my career. I had to buy the Archibald Press within the next two weeks or my option would be forfeit. In order to do so I needed every penny of cash I could raise. *All* my assets had to be liquid, including this place in Davenport Road. I had a buyer and the price was right. Any hold-up now would be fatal.

I veered away from that word. I approached Teddy. He was naked under the sheet, but round his shoulders he was wearing the Sulka dressing-gown my mother had given me. I should have to do something about that or there would be questions asked. Approaching ninety, and more than able to remember, she gave me the dressing-gown in 1954.

I went to the window and looked out. Darkness would have been a help, but it was solid, steady daylight, and there were some hours of the day yet to run and no news of an eclipse.

I relaxed on my heels in the squatting posture and opened my mouth to breathe deep in the lion position.

146

Ten deep breaths to calm me down. I saw a dead lion once. It was lying on its side in a field outside a circus tent. The trainer said it had died of a heart attack.

Ten deep lion breaths and I still felt the same: nervous but resolved. I suppose that *is* courage, really, to fear what you are going to do and yet go on to do it.

I went over to the bed and drew back the sheet. There was a fair amount of blood. I can stand blood, though, it does not make me squeamish, but it introduced a disposal problem. I could never send *those* sheets to the laundry. They would have to go with him. 'Oh Teddy,' I thought, 'why *here*? And who did it? And why?' I was trying to keep an open mind on this question, which I did not regard as my affair. I've been a perfectly legitimate businessman all my working life, but I've been around enough to see murder done, one way or another, more than once.

From the ceiling came a series of staccato little bangs. This did not worry me. I knew what it was. Mrs Delacour above has a pekinese dog, a well behaved beast, but when it gets angry it bangs on the floor with its little back paw. That was the noise I was hearing now.

I began to shake a little, all the same. The truth was I was thoroughly scared. It was another reason for getting the body out of there. I didn't want to be the next one found dead here, and it seemed to me it might happen. I have seen men die, I was a soldier once, but I've never been at home to it before. A year ago I had given Teddy the keys of my flat for a week's stay and this is what I got for it. I didn't know why he had moved in without asking this time, and I did not want to find out. The answer could only be painful and might be dangerous.

I went round the place, tidying up and gathering up his possessions, which were scattered about everywhere. His own bunch of keys was on my desk. By degrees I put

147

together an outfit of clothes for him. I laid everything ready on a chair by the bed.

I knew I'd have to dress him. He couldn't go out of the room as he was, could he? But before I did that, I did a surprising thing. Well, it surprised me anyway.

He had faint black stubble showing, so I shaved him, and after I had shaved him, I put some after-shave lotion on him. That was what surprised me, putting on the after-shave. The shaving itself seemed just something I had to do. The lotion was an extra, a sort of lustral rite.

All the time I was dressing him, shirt, pants, collar and tie, I was thinking about Marie Vetsera.

You know about Marie Vetsera? She was the girl the Archduke Rudolph took along with him on his suicide ride to Mayerling. After she was dead they dressed her body, even to its hat and furs, and then, on the Emperor's orders, they drove her through the back lanes of the villages in a carriage, propped up between her two uncles, to her secret burial-place, so that anyone seeing her would think that she was alive. For the honour of the Emperor.

The door-bell rang just as I was finishing. It rang again quickly so that I knew it would be best to answer. I closed the bedroom door and wished I could lock it.

The pekinese from upstairs stood on my threshold, lead trailing.

'Oh, little friend,' I said sadly, looking down on him. 'Go away home.'

The boy that Mrs Delacour hired to take him for a walk appeared from the shadows.

'You're letting him get out of control,' I said. 'Ringing the door-bell and all.'

'He *made* me do it.' He showed me an ankle with a sweet set of teeth marks, just a graze but with the promise of more to come if necessary. 'He's in a rotten mood. He wants to see you.'

The truth is we've all spoilt the little creature shockingly, and he thinks he can do what he likes. Now he was barking.

'He knows you're back, you see,' said the boy. 'He could smell you. He's excited.'

'Yes. I just got back,' I said, feeling distracted by the noise. The dog pushed past me, ran to the bedroom door and clawed at it with his hard front paws. Before I could get there the door had swung open a small distance. The dog stood there barking.

'He's barking at the man in the room,' said the boy.

'What man?'

'The man in the hat that's sitting in there.'

'There's no one in there.'

'The *dead* man,' he explained.

'He's not dead.'

'He *looks* dead.'

'There's no man in there and he's not dead,' I said, hastily collecting the dog and pushing them both outside the door.

I leaned against it, breathing heavily. How could I have guessed that the paw pounding on the floor above would mean such bad luck for me?

Sooner or later the boy would tell his mother or Mrs Delacour what he had seen. The only thing was that he was such a liar that no one would believe him, while the dog, a much more reliable witness, was, happily, in no position to speak.

After I had got Teddy nicely dressed I let him lie back on the bed. His body was loose and floppy, so I guessed he was over rigor mortis, as it is called. Perhaps I should say here that he had a wound in the side of his head near the right temple. I had, in fact, covered it with a hat, as my visitor had pointed out. So now you know why Teddy was wearing a hat.

He looked peaceful, as if he had gone out without hearing the one that got him. They say you do, although it must be hard to check on that one. And I thought how funny it would be if he'd died of heart failure at the very moment he'd shot himself through the brain.

The mattress and bedclothes I rolled up in a long flat sausage without letting myself take a good look. I thought for a moment that I could put fresh linen on the bed and start again from there, but it was no good, I knew the bed would have to go.

The parts unscrew easily and I had it in four pieces, including the mattress, in ten minutes. It could be stored in the garage while I decided what to do with it. It is a valuable object and the Musée des Beaux Arts in Paris had shown an interest. I thought I would give it to them. One way and another, it deserved to go on show. And it would be safely out of the country.

Before carrying it out to the garage, I peeped through the kitchen window and it was just as well I did so, because the dog was out there on the step, lead dangling, eyes bright and hopeful.

The boy was not far away, of course, standing on tiptoe trying to see in through the bedroom window. He could not quite make it.

I beckoned him over. 'You know the dead man you thought you saw?'

He nodded.

'He was killed by the Mafia. You've heard of the Mafia?'

He nodded again.

'If you go to the Park you will see two cars drawn up in the road. That's them. They are waiting. A few yards round the corner you will see two more cars. That is the police. They are waiting, too. In a little while they are going to shoot it out. If you go along you could watch.'

He looked at me for a moment. He had a good head-piece on him, and he wondered. Then he said: 'I'm going that way anyway.'

'Good.' I watched him move off, then I called him back. 'Don't forget the dog.'

In the end I carried Teddy to my car in the garage. I picked him up like a child and carried him in my arms. 'For the honour of the Emperor, the honour of the Emperor,' I muttered. It's stupid bits of play-acting like that that help you through.

As we drove past the park, with Teddy sitting in the back, hardly visible through the small back windows, I saw the boy. He was walking slowly past a row of parked cars, stopping to stare in each one as he passed.

Teddy had lived over a garage, which simplified the next part of my task. I stopped the car, opened the garage doors, drove in, shut the doors, then carried Teddy up to his own bed and placed him in it, where at least he was at home. The place looked squalid and uncared for. I un-packed his case and placed his possessions naturally around. Then, moved by one of the silliest impulses I've had, I cleaned up the flat and put the milk bottles out.

I put the hat on my head, I don't know why, got in the car and drove myself home.

I parked the car in my own garage and walked into my kitchen through the back door. As soon as I was inside the door-bell rang.

I went to open it. There stood Mrs Delacour and I knew at once that the boy had spoken.

'Oh, good evening, I just wanted to, that is, the boy said . . .' she began, looking flustered. I saw her eyes take in the hat on my head and her expression changed. 'That is, I don't think there was anything in it. He was just fibbing as usual.'

'That's right,' I said. 'Just fibbing again. Excuse me now, please.'

I went straight to my office and got down to work. I took one or two phone calls. Later, I returned to my flat with the pleasant feeling that I would not be disturbed there. I remember I had to lock the kitchen window, which, stupidly, I must have left unlocked.

During the next few days I started the arrangements for selling my flat and setting up my business deal. All went smoothly. Three days after I had arrived I had a shock. There was a letter for me in Teddy's writing. For a terrible moment I wondered if he was not dead after all, but I soon realized what had happened. He had sent the letter by second-class mail and the Post Office had taken a long while to deliver. I think Teddy may have counted on this delay.

After I had read the letter I put it carefully in the pocket next to my heart to keep it safe. They would have to kill me to get at it. After all, I owed Teddy something.

But the arrival of this letter meant that for me Teddy was neither quite living nor quite dead.

Then, sooner than I had expected, Teddy's body was found. He was dead all right. I held my breath, but I was undisturbed. Until one evening, returning alone, having said good-bye for ever to Flynn, I found a man in my garage. Not dead this time, fully alive, and prepared to be aggressive.

The body of the man found shot dead in his flat over a garage in Windmill Road was identified by his landlord, who owned the sweet shop next door, as his tenant Theodore Drysdale. For various reasons the police who came to the flat to investigate decided that the name Theodore (which means 'god-given') and Drysdale were false names. They decided this because in the flat they found a bill from a cheap hotel made out to T. Drury, and in a drawer a dry-cleaning tag with the name Darley scrawled on it. The hotel was in Kensington where it begins to be seedy, the dry-cleaners was south of the river at Camberwell, and Windmill Road where Drysdale-Drury-Darley lay dead was in Hammersmith. All of which suggested he had moved around.

A more accurate identification became necessary and work began on this while they awaited the results of the post mortem. They took the fingerprints of the dead man and tried to match them with any prints of known criminals. But apparently he was not a convicted criminal.

His wanderings, however, suggested someone on the run. His few possessions, such as they were, appeared to be of good quality and fairly new. There was no food, but about fifty pounds in cash. If he was not a criminal he might have been the associate of criminals. He began to appear like a man who might have been the treasurer or writer of an organized gang. All high-class gangs like to have such a figure; he gives them lustre and a sense of efficiency, in much the same way as a good secretary does to any business. The level of education required need not be high. Several things about the dead man suggested quite a good education. He had a copy of Solzhenitsyn's *August 1914*, which is not everyone's reading. Two copies of *The Scientific American* were on a table. By the bed was *The Sirens of Titan* and a paper-back edition of Lilian Ross's *Picture*. He was literate, anyway, however educated. But what made him look like a criminal was the terrible shoddiness of the life he had been leading.

In an exercise in lateral thinking the police then directed their attention to Olivia Cooper. Lateral thinking is no new process for the police. Indeed, suspicion is a lateral and not a deductive act of cognition. Olivia

Cooper was not the only person caught in the net of lateral thinking. In addition, there was a man who had reported seeing a body lying half in and half out of a telephone-box in a road near Paddington Station. He might be a suspect. There was also an elderly woman who claimed she had seen a man shot dead in the Park at Deptford and she actually had the gun to show them. One shot had gone from it, too. She might be worth following up.

But Olivia was far and away the most interesting possibility, with her circumstantial and puzzling story.

Lateral thinking travels best by hearsay and rumour, and emerges triumphantly from discussions that are ostensibly about something else. There was a meeting called in a room in the new buildings of New Scotland Yard to discuss the security arrangements for a visit to London from the new leader of China. Both Idden and Coffin were present, Idden sitting at the back of the room and looking secretive. He came over at the end and said a word or two to Coffin. Nothing very much, his words sounded quite friendly, but Coffin recognized them as his quietus. He would soon be given the chance of a quiet retirement. And if he refused?

It was at this moment, when he was receiving the news that his career was over, that he started to think about the man found shot dead in Windmill Road above a garage. He asked himself if the man could be fitted into Olivia's story. He was dead, he had been shot and he had not, so far, been fitted out with a killer. In other words, he was available.

Coffin asked for and received a transcript of Olivia's tale. He knew the story, but seeing it in black and white made a difference. Some points stood out, just as they always had done.

Olivia had said the man she called Timothy Dean was alive one minute, then dead and rigid the next.

It was as if, for Timothy, the natural processes of death and corruption had been speeded up.

'The film is out of sync,' Olivia had cried to herself.

'And as there was no body we naturally thought she was nuts,' said Coffin. 'It was easier for us not to believe her, so we didn't.' He sighed. 'And, of course, it's *not* true. But if you accept that something has gone wrong with time, then it is true.

'The man was shot dead. The body was caught at once in a state of cadaveric spasm. Common enough in a violent death. This is Olivia's first description.

'Then she saw that the body fluids had settled, thus causing bruises and stains. This is her second description. The two descriptions relate to two different stages, so something has gone wrong with time, with Olivia's time. Her clock has gone wrong. Under some emotional pressure she has telescoped two episodes.'

Lateral thinking then led him to consider garages, and the uses they might have for violent men. He sat there thinking about garages. What he was thinking about interested him, but, take it all in all, his mood was bad.

Chapter Eleven

Timothy Dean saw the man in his garage and thought: 'Here we go again. This time it's my turn.'

One man at the end of his tether always knows another, and these two men knew each other.

'Funny thing,' said Dean, in his beautiful voice. 'I thought I was doing fine till I saw you.' He slammed the car door 'Crazy, crazy.' He took a deep breath. 'I suppose I always knew you would come. Why me, I might say, but it wouldn't do any good, would it? You'd kill me first and apologize afterwards, whatever I said.'

'Why should I kill you?'

'Rhetorical question, I suppose, to give you time to get the gun out? If I sound brave, pretend it's not me. Just get it over fast.' He was swallowing hard. 'Don't worry, I won't struggle. I'm a fatalist.'

In spite of his calm voice, his colour was bad.

There was a dead silence.

'You're going to do it yourself, are you, and not get the woman to do it for you?'

'No. I'll do my own killing. Such as it is.'

'Someone will hear the shot and come running,' said Dean despairingly. 'But I suppose you don't care.'

'Come inside the house and we'll talk there.'

'Oh yes. What does it matter to me? And when the talking is over what shall you say to me then? "Lie down and I'll kill you"?'

'Go inside.'

When they were inside the lovely sitting-room, which bore signs of being dismantled, the younger, tougher-looking man motioned to the other to sit down.

'So you're moving out,' he said, looking round.

'That's right.'

'I came just in time, then.'

The other was silent. Then he burst out: 'I knew as soon as I saw the letter it was dynamite.'

The other man considered, then said, 'Show me the letter.'

Timothy Dean got up, went to his desk, got out a letter still in its envelope, and threw it over. 'That's what you want, isn't it? The letter of a gunman. A gunman who never fired a gun.'

The other man opened the letter and read it aloud:

'Dear Cousin Tim,

'I'm in a bad way and I think I am going to be killed. I'm frightened about that, Tim, as I think you would be.'

The reader raised his eyes from the letter and looked at Tim, who was sitting on a pale leather chair with his eyes closed. He went back to his reading.

'If I am killed, I want the killer to get his. That's vindictive but I *am* vindictive. So I'm going to write this all out formally, like a confession, and you can do what you like with it.'

'More fool than I am, I kept the letter,' said Dean. 'How did you know about it?'

No answer, the fellow was still reading.

'I shall sign this Teddy Driscoll but whether that is my true name or not I shall never know. My mother came back from America to her family when I was two years old, calling herself a widow. The Widow Driscoll. She remarried when I was eight, a prosperous businessman with two sons

157

and a dead wife of his own. They were both killed in a car crash when I was fifteen, leaving me a little money, a good education and a disastrous constitution. "It'll go badly with you if you come up with a bad illness, for you've no constitution at all," our family doctor said, and he was about right.'

'You can forget that about his mother and it not being his real name,' interrupted Timothy Dean. 'That's all a tale. He was Driscoll all right, but he liked to make it more romantic.'

'Are you telling me he was a liar?'

'No, not a liar. But he couldn't help telling a tale. You ought to know. He was one of you, wasn't he? But he couldn't do any killing.'

The other man looked at him thoughtfully before returning to his reading.

'You know, it has just struck me that I am writing my obituary. It does not fall to everyone to do this, so I would like to get some matters straight from the beginning. I am a coward. I'm glad I've said that: it takes a weight off my shoulders to know that, after all, I am not guilty of anything except being human.'

A few moments passed. Timothy Dean moved restlessly.

'Having a bit of money was a bad thing. It gave me freedom and put me among men who were willing to use my freedom. After leaving school I went, as you well know, Timothy, since you recommended it, to study at Trinity College, Dublin. The family business and my home were in the north but the south attracted me. I was there for two years in which I did not do much work but during which I joined an organization called Sons of Erin, it was a pseudonym, really, for a more violent Association, and it was named after Johnny MacNeill. I was proud of joining at the time. I thought I was noble.'

'I don't know anything,' said Timothy Dean, suddenly. 'If you've got any idea of knocking me about, torture and so on, there's no point. He didn't confide in *me* and, if he got away with anything, then he didn't tell me.'

'Just keep quiet, please,' said the other man, with a steady, cold good humour.

'I had no intention of killing; I went in on the administrative side. I was a finance officer. There didn't seem much to it. It was a shock when I realized I would have to join in an act of violence or be punished. We all had to be equally guilty, you see. I hadn't grasped that fact: I thought I could do the good things and let someone else do the bad. It did not work out that way. I won't talk about it. But after it I left Ireland .,.'

The reader raised his head. 'I've got to the bit where he ran away.'

Timothy Dean winced.

'Take no notice of anything that has been said. It is all a lie. I did not take their money with me.'

The reader raised his head from the document. 'It breaks off there,' he said, 'as if interrupted.'

'I told you there was nothing,' said Timothy Dean, in a dull voice.

'But there *is* one last paragraph addressed to you.'

Scrawled across the bottom in an unsteady hand, it read:

'Oh, Timmy, because you love me ... I met this girl in the train and when she looked at me and smiled I thought I would get her to stay with me and she would protect me. Perhaps they wouldn't kill me if she was there. Or at the worst, we would go together.

'It is very terrible, Timmy, to go out alone: I wanted company on the way.'

It was not the last sentence of all. One more remained to be read.

'I think now, Timmy, that the girl was sent to kill me.'

The girl was sent to kill me. The girl was sent to kill me. The girl was the gun.

The reader looked across to Timothy Dean. 'I think I ought to tell you that I am a policeman.'

'I've been thinking that for the last five minutes.'

'I came here to look for a bed.'

'It's in the garage. Made for me by Stephen Foster-James and it cost me two hundred pounds ... I moved the body. I don't know how you found out. Daft, wasn't it? Do you know who the girl was who killed him? I'd like her to be caught.'

'I expect she will be,' said John Coffin. 'We know her name. She even told us about it, in a garbled kind of way.'

Chapter Twelve

Olivia Cooper, stand forward to receive justice. You told your story and it was false.

Olivia had told her own story and had told it badly, so that her friends were left incredulous. She had led those who listened to her up to a blank wall and confronted them with a *trompe l'oeil*.

For a moment it looked as though her story and John Coffin's would diverge, as her second husband's and hers already had. But the fact was that all the time there had been another story welded to Olivia's. In Olivia's recounting, this plot had been virtually edited out. If it was a film, you would have said that a lot of the action lay on the cutting-room floor.

But now a new character was to appear. His was the face on the cutting-room floor.

Detective Inspector Idden had brought him in, together with one other man and a middle-aged woman. It was an arrest which had delighted Idden's heart, as it was in a professionally proper style. Idden was a purist and, secretly, a follower of Inspector Lestrade, for whom he had every respect as opposed to the insufferable Holmes. It was a good many years since he had actually read the stories of Sherlock Holmes. At the same time he had also been a student of Sexton Blake and his assistant, Ginger. Dick Tracy had come later. He thought he had forgotten these indulgences of his boyhood, but they were still there, colouring his approach to his work. Unconsciously he had admitted that the policeman is always the inferior animal and must keep his end up by military precision and bearing, leaving real 'smartness' to the other operators.

The three people he had arrested for the armed robbery with violence in Creamery Road were professionally committed to silence. They would not confess, would barely even acknowledge their names. Secretive, surly, and, underneath, scared men. The woman had got herself out of the situation by going into a diabetic coma. Apart from a priest and a doctor she had seen no one.

To Idden's pleasure, the three bandits had been arrested by straight professional police work. They were on a list of those known to be in the south of England; one of the men was suspected of having arranged a similar robbery in Belfast; the finger-print and palm-print of the other man had been found on the counter of the robbed post office and on the handbrake of Olivia's car, and, finally, Idden had an informer placed in the lodging-house where the men and the woman had been living. It was not necessary for the men to speak; Idden felt he could speak for them.

There was no evidence to connect Olivia Cooper with this act of violence, except the use of her car.

In a decayed-looking house behind a church the rooms in which the three arrested people had lived were searched. In them were found a scatter of personal possessions and clothes, nothing valuable. A box of ammunition for a Webley 0.32 was found in the men's room; in the woman's was a hypodermic syringe and a small bottle of liquid. No gun was found.

The ammuntion was at once identified as being of the same calibre as that used by the weapon fired in Creamery Road. The bottle contained insulin, which is used in the treatment of diabetes, as well as having other uses.

A watch was kept on Olivia Cooper, but she was behaving normally. Then the body of the shot man was found and, according to orthodox police methods, identified as Edward (Teddy) Driscoll, known to the police to be hiding in London. His next of kin, an uncle, was informed. After a short delay, the uncle identified the body and, casually, mentioned his other nephew, Timothy Dean, who lived in Davenport Road.

By this time the post mortem on Teddy Driscoll had been completed. The bullet found in his skull proved to have come from a Webley 0.32 automatic pistol. There was a delay of a day before this bullet was matched against the bullet found at Creamery Road, but when the comparison was made the appearance of the grooves suggested that the same gun had been used. The decay of the body tissues ruled out tests to see if powder burns were present. But, in the absence of the weapon, murder had to be presumed.

So the wheel had turned, and the story of one set of characters was seen to complement the story of another group. It was Olivia's story and Teddy's story and the story of the three who had been arrested. It all depended on where you were standing.

Olivia had told her story badly. That is, she had told it like a human being, as it happened to her. In the telling of every tale there is some mechanical contrivance which turns a chronicle into a plot. In Olivia's case it was a bottle and a hypodermic syringe.

Olivia had told her story badly, and yet it had not prevented Coffin feeling for her an emotion akin to love. He saw that Olivia would always have this power of summoning up emotions. He went to see her with the idea of making things easy for her. He wanted to see her, look at her face and say good-bye.

It was surprising, therefore, that he found himself paying all his outstanding bills, checking his passport, and

163

changing six hundred pounds sterling into francs and lire.

'Of course, I'm not running away,' he would have said if you'd asked. 'There's nowhere to run to.'

All the same, he was quietly and expeditiously making his arrangements to depart. A letter of resignation was typed, signed, and in his pocket.

By the time he got to see Olivia and was face to face with her, the words were tumbling out of his mouth.

She stood in the centre of her sitting-room, which, in its casual muddle, looked exactly as he had last seen it, and stared at him silently. She looked more beautiful and strangely more substantial than when they had last met. He realized that she had actually put on some weight. Women were strange creatures.

'You look better than I expected,' he said.

'Oh yes. I've stopped flinching when the telephone rings. I open the door even to strangers and I am putting in a full day's work at the office.' Her tone was dry. Along with her despairs, Olivia had lost her fears. She seemed at peace.

I suppose, thought Coffin, she's done the worst thing she could ever be asked to do, she has killed, and underneath she has faced up to it. He wondered if her intention was to kill herself.

'How's the memory?'

Olivia turned aside to light a cigarette. 'Coming on. I believe if I leaned on it everything would come back.'

'I don't want you to stay here,' he heard himself say. 'Pack it in and clear out.'

Olivia gave a small shake of the head. It might have meant dissent, or it might have been amusement. With incredulity he saw it *was* amusement.

'I've stopped running,' she said briefly. 'I've stopped everything. I just eat, drink, and breathe.'

'That won't keep you going long.'

164

'I'm doing marvellously.'

To his amazement he saw it was true.

'Twenty-odd years in prison and you won't be doing so marvellously,' he said.

Her gaze just flicked towards him, and her expression hardly altered. She was beyond minding the odd, cruel blow.

'Sorry,' he said.

'It's nothing.'

'You *did* kill him?'

'I'm afraid I must have done,' she said in a serious voice.

'If you imagine I shall enjoy living twenty years outside with you inside, you're wrong.'

'I've been thinking and thinking about it,' said Olivia. 'And I really can't see it any other way. I *must* have killed him. Why? I suppose you are asking why did a nice girl like Olivia do such a thing?'

'I wasn't asking, but I'd like to know.'

She looked away, as if she was seeing those men who had got her off the train travelling to Euston and transferred her to a train on the way to a more terrible destination. They. 'The only person who could really answer that was Teddy Driscoll himself. We were both deep in something we couldn't get away from, and we were both dead frightened. Kill? I didn't mean to kill any more than he meant to kill, and steal, and run away, but he did it, and so, it seems, did I. My *task*, or what I was asked to do, was to identify him. To find out if the man living in Davenport Road was really Teddy Driscoll. When I visited him there he almost convinced me he was Timothy Dean. But he never really seemed at *home* in the place. And by and by, as he told me more about himself, I *knew*. I knew who he was all right. And we were both in the same boat. Do you know that bit in a film where the hero is

165

given a gun and has to shoot either his best friend or himself? It's to prove which side he is on. That's how it was for me and Teddy.'

'Were you threatened with violence yourself?' asked Coffin. 'I suppose you were.' He was thinking that it might be used in her defence.

'I knew what I'd get if I didn't behave. I was beaten up a little once, on the stair where I lived. That was because I was slow . . . But Teddy and I were drawing together . . . We had so much in common, you see.'

At this moment her telephone gave two rings and then stopped. Then it rang twice again.

Coffin looked at Olivia.

'It's a signal,' she said. 'So I know to answer. Otherwise I let it ring.' She picked it up. 'Hello, Tony.' She listened. He saw her face lose colour and her lips tighten. Then she put down the receiver.

So it's come, he thought, this is the moment. 'Come on,' he said impatiently. 'What is it?'

'Tony says one of his contacts has just rung him to say that a warrant has just been sworn out for my arrest.'

'Why *now*?' said Coffin, still enough of a policeman to wonder who this contact, not himself, could be.

'Tony's not sure. He thinks they've just decided that I will confess. I expect I will, too.' Her colour was coming back, but the skin on her face looked tight, as if the flesh below had altered its nature.

'Yes, it could be,' said Coffin. He knew Idden's way of waiting, then suddenly gathering his forces and pouncing.

Olivia sat down and let her hands rest in her lap. 'They may be here any minute. It was good of Tony to let me know. But, of course, he enjoys it. It makes his life interesting.'

'Pity they found a box of ammunition,' Coffin said vindictively.

166

'A box of ammunition and a syringe and a bottle of insulin and a lot of dirty underclothes, Tony said.' Olivia's voice managed a faint dry amusement. 'No gun. They think I must have that.'

'A bottle of *what*?'

'Insulin. The woman with them, Anny Grey, was a diabetic.'

'You don't know much, do you?'

'What do you mean?' In spite of herself she caught his excitement. She stood up.

'Get your things on. We're going out.'

'No. I must stay.'

But he was already bringing her coat and throwing it over her shoulders. 'Move.'

'Where am I going?'

'Over the hills and far away.' He was delighted with himself.

'Am I coming back?' Olivia grabbed her handbag.

'If I had my way you'd never come back here. But from where we are going now, yes, we shall be returning.'

'But what's it all about?' She was panting after him as he hurried down the narrow stairs to the front door. There was no elegance and not much privacy where Olivia lived: the front door stood open already.

'It's all in your own account. You tell about a parcel. You tell about the attack on you. It's what you've left out, Olivia, that's going to count.'

Coffin drove fast and Olivia sat silently. Then she said: 'Oh but . . .'

'Keep quiet.'

'But this is Davenport Road.'

The car stopped, he hurried her out and dragged her across the pavement.

'Oh goodness,' said Olivia.

Timothy Dean opened the door to them. 'Oh, hello. You again.' He looked surprised.

'Not gone yet, then?' said Coffin.

'Tomorrow. Well, come in.' He looked curiously at Olivia. She saw a tall, slender man wearing a pale tweed suit with a matching waistcoat. There was something about his features that reminded her of Teddy. Her eyes filled with tears. 'I'm moving things out now.'

Coffin did not wait to introduce Olivia, but pressed on. 'Have you moved the things in the garage?'

'The bed?' He shuddered slightly. 'No.'

'Oh no, no,' cried Olivia, and covered her eyes. Coffin dragged her hands away from her face and, tugging her after him, hurried her out of the back door and down towards the garage. She was vaguely aware of Timothy Dean following them and exclaiming aloud.

'This you have to do,' said Coffin to Olivia.

'You're punishing me,' she gasped.

'Yes, and no.' He was already pulling aside the wrappings in which the mattress had been rolled.

Like a tongue it uncurled before them, pillows and sheets spreading themselves out on the floor. A blotch of blood stained one quarter of the sheet.

Olivia moaned. She closed her eyes. She heard Coffin talking in an urgent voice and then heard Timothy Dean give a loud exclamation.

'Don't touch it,' said Coffin. *'Don't touch it.'*

She opened her eyes. 'It's a gun.'

'Yes, the gun. It was caught up in the bedding.'

'I didn't know it was there,' said Dean. 'I didn't see it . . . I rolled everything up with my eyes closed.'

'Leave it.' He turned towards Olivia. 'You told your story badly, but with the help of this gun and a bottle of insulin I shall try to tell it better. I'm going to make a telephone call. Come and listen to me make it.'

168

Timothy Dean and Olivia Cooper listened together as he spoke on the telephone.

'Idden? I am in Davenport Road. Yes, you know where. I have something here to interest you. A gun.' There was a moment's silence, while he listened. 'It will require a little ratiocination on your part. That's another word for thinking. About Edward Driscoll. He killed himself. Yes, *felo de se*. Take this gun and get it tested. There will be no fingerprints but his found on it. I think you will find the gun was sent to him. Probably in a parcel.'

It sounded to the two listeners as if Inspector Idden was asking anxious, hurried questions. Then it was over.

'He's going to take some convincing,' said Coffin, with satisfaction. 'But, by God, he'd better be convinced.'

'And what about me?' questioned Olivia. 'What about me? What do you suppose my part was?' She was shaking. 'What, in the end, do you suppose I did?'

'What was it I did? What happened to me?' Olivia was still asking the question even some hours later, after Idden had visited the house in Davenport Road, after statements had been taken from all three who witnessed the gun being found, and after she had been allowed to go home.

Olivia was the dual character in her own story, tragedy, melodrama, whichever it was, and she wanted to know the plot.

'It was like you said, Olivia: the film was out of sync.' He had not taken her home, but to a bar where they could eat. It was a run-down, empty place, exactly suited to his mood. Exhilaration had gone. Exhaustion had arrived.

'Insulin, as well as treating diabetes, was once used as a shock treatment. It affects the mind powerfully, liberating the tongue and producing patches of amnesia. I believe you were given a dose, on the stairs, in your own house,

169

the night you were attacked, to make you talk. You were no longer trusted to tell the truth unaided.'

Olivia stared, and then looked down at her wrists.

'You *do* remember something of it. You always have.'

She nodded. 'Yes . . . Finding out about Sarah and my husband was a shock, too, although I hate to admit it.'

The bar where they sat was dark and quiet, but she could look outside the window and see the world outside hurrying by.

'It's frightening,' she said. 'To think a part of me peeled off then, acted, spoke, gave an account of what it was doing and went wandering off and has not yet come home. Where is that Olivia and what is she doing now? She's there somewhere, the Olivia who knew that Teddy had killed himself and couldn't face up to it.'

'I should bury her,' said Coffin comfortably. 'She was a foolish, foolish girl.'

Olivia shook her head sadly and then sipped her drink. It's easy for him, she was thinking, look at him, he's all in one piece, isn't he?

Distantly she seemed to hear a man's voice saying: Good-bye Olivia, kiss me good-bye. It's better to kill yourself than wait to be killed. Come with me, Olivia, will you? Let's go together, a bullet each, that's high romance, my love.

With an effort she wrenched her mind back to the present. 'I ran away,' she said wonderingly. 'I ran away because I didn't want to get killed. I wanted to live.' She sounded thoroughly surprised at herself. 'What a bad joke.'

'Olivia,' said Coffin firmly. 'You've *always* wanted to live.'

So Olivia's story would always have a hole in it, because one Olivia was gone for ever. Or almost for ever.

170

Little by little the knot that held the characters together relaxed its hold and they moved away, to fresh knots, fresh stories.

Idden went off home to his wife and saw his children. 'No, quite a good day. Nothing special. Let's go to bed early.' He didn't even know there *was* more than one story. No imagination, Idden.

Sarah and Olivia's second husband wandered off, hand in hand together. Well, more or less. For them it was a love story.

For Teddy a tragedy, for his cousin Timothy a black comedy.

Lally was an exception. A lot more to tell there, one day, some day. Lally's story had not happened yet. Lally was a story going round for a plot to happen to it.

For himself, John Coffin was unsure. Perhaps you knew what your story was truly about when it was over. And he was not sure if his story was yet over. Perhaps there was going to be another chapter or two.

But with Olivia staring at him now across her drink, wondering how *her* story was going to end, he had to do something.

All unhappy stories have a different ending, all happy stories end in the same way.

He kissed her.

'Yes, that's a classic ending.' She looked appreciative. 'And I'd like to stay with it. I really would. It would be good. But an even better ending is the surprise one. And I have a surprise for you.'

Coffin looked at her.

'There's something I have to tell you. I really did kill Teddy. He had the gun and he wanted us to have a suicide pact. He was going to kill me and then himself. I expect he would have done it, too. I could just picture him sitting there for hours holding my hand and crying over me, before getting up the nerve to join me. If he ever did. But that isn't me.

'It was my job, as you know, to confirm his identity, and to leave the rest to the killers. Well, I proved not to have much stomach for that sort of thing.' Her tone was bitter. 'I didn't know what to do. He was in trouble, however you looked at it. I didn't want him to die but I suddenly heard myself say: "You're quite right. It will be easier if you do it yourself." I remember his eyes when I said that. He knew I was right, that was the terrible thing. And so, before I could say anything else, he turned the gun ...' She stopped for a moment. 'I wasn't lying when I said I didn't know what happened. I fainted, I think. I did forget. For a while that moment was obliterated. I suppose the drug I had been given helped create confusion. But gradually I remembered a little at a time. The picture kept coming back, each time a little more was added.

'The whole tale has been a bit like that, hasn't it? Each time round with the merry-go-round the truth stands out better.'

'I'd like to just sit speechless,' said Coffin slowly, 'but there's a bit more yet, isn't there?'

She put out her hand and took his. 'I'm a coward like Teddy, always remember that, but I'm not asking you to come too.'

'What's that?' His voice was difficult to control, and came out nastier and louder than he had meant.

'I don't have to worry about punishment or twenty years inside. I won't be around to know. I went to a hospital in Middlesex the week-end before I got in that train to Euston. The week-end I *didn't* stay with my sister. They did some special tests there on me. A boy from the village I grew up in is a specialist in this hospital. I had to put up quite a smoke screen for my sister and with my brother-

172

in-law to prevent her guessing, but I think she guessed all the same. The result of the tests came a few days ago to my doctor. But I knew already. I had a letter directly from my friend saying I must go into hospital soon. I have a type of cancer.'

There was a moment of silence, during which the bar was dark and quiet, with even the barman sound asleep.

'That's a hard thing to take in at short notice,' said her companion. He had moved further back into the alcove where they were sitting, so that she could hardly make out his face. He could have been anyone. 'That's not how I want to end the tale. I believe in hope. I don't accept despair. I'm for life. I want to end with the feeling that there's more to come on another page.'

He reached out and gently held both her hands. There was another silence, then Olivia laughed. To her intense satisfaction she found she was experiencing real amusement. It was like the splinter melting on the Ice Queen's heart. 'Yes,' she said. 'Yes, I know. I'll turn up as the Space Age Princess in another time on another planet. Or I'll turn out to be immortal or something. Lucky lucky me.'

The door of the bar opened and a party of laughing people came in. The noise of the city came in with them, the noise of people laughing, crying, sneezing, yawning, belching, getting born and dying.

There was a different ending for everyone. You put your hand into the lucky dip and came up with something.

CHCS 20